Praise For ...g's First Collection
The Truly Needy And Other Stories
(University of Pittsburgh Press)

"Convincing detail and candid, insightful narrative draw the reader deep into the lives of these ordinary people and their sometimes extraordinary revelations. Honig...permeates the collection with a quirky hopefulness in the resilience of these memorable characters and their unexpected moments of human connection—even as they struggle, with quiet heroism, to make their place in a modern world they can neither control nor explain."

Publisher's Weekly

"...Honig's stories brim over with memorable characters, enough rich details from modern life to fill a novel, and a heart big enough to embrace the world in all its complexity and ambiguity. *The Truly Needy* is, in a word, one of the most satisfying literary works of the '90s, one loaded with gifts readers will remember for a long, long time."

**National Book Award Winner
Charles Johnson**

continued

"Lucy Honig's work possesses a startling, unnerving moral energy; it is work that tells us a good deal about who we are—work that addresses darker moments, and yet, does so without moralistic bombast—rather, with a talented writer's illuminating, disarming irony."

Robert Coles

"It's too bad that so-called serious fiction has such a narrow following, for there are few of us who do not truly need the use of [Lucy Honig's] ears and eyes, the brush of her hand."

Indianapolis Star

Open Season

Other Scala House Titles

Guarding Hanna
by Miha Mazzini

Whole New Religion
by Bob Jakubovic

Open Season
...
STORIES BY LUCY HONIG

[signature: Lucy Honig]

SCALA HOUSE PRESS
Seattle

OPEN SEASON COPYRIGHT ©2002 BY LUCY HONIG

All rights reserved. No part of this book may be reproduced in any form or by any electronic or mechanical means, including information storage and retrieval systems, without permission in writing from the publisher, except by a reviewer who may quote brief passages in a review.

FIRST NORTH AMERICAN EDITION 2002

This is a work of fiction. Names, places, characters, and incidents are either products of the author's imagination or are used fictitiously.

ISBN:0-9720287-2-2

SCALA HOUSE PUBLISHERS, LLC
PO BOX 17964
SEATTLE, WASHINGTON 98107
WWW.SCALAHOUSEPRESS.COM

Type Set In Electra

COVER DESIGN BY KEVIN BERGER, GRAPHITI ASSOCIATES
WWW.GRAPHITI.COM

COVER PHOTOGRAPH COURTESY OF GETTY IMAGES
WWW.GETTYIMAGES.COM

PRINTED IN CANADA

The author would like to extend her deep gratitude to Ledig House, Hawthornden Castle International Retreat for Writers, and Le Chateau de Lavigny International Writers' Colony, for their generous gifts of time, space, and peace.

Contents

Open Season	3
The Story	79
Josephine's Release	93
Bobbi and Loretta	105
The Menorah Girl	121
Acknowledgments	145
About the Author	147

For my mother and the Polenberg legacy

OPEN SEASON

1. *Nobody'll Ever Bother You Back There*

THE FIRST SUMMER, THE SUMMER of 1973, our mailbox got shot.

At the beginning they only stole the mail. Sometimes they put our mail in somebody else's box and other times they put somebody else's mail in our box, but mostly they just stole it, down at the end of the road a mile from where we were building the house. So we put a lock on the mailbox. Three days later we found the box, wrenched off its post and crumpled up in the ditch, with four bullet holes in it.

"Sounds to me," said the postmaster, "like the fellow who shot up a barn last year." But he wouldn't say who.

We thought of Stanley, who seemed like someone who could shoot up a barn but not like someone who would shoot a mailbox. We asked him. He *had* shot the barn. But we never did find out who shot the mailbox.

We lived in a tiny shack while we built the house. One night earlier that summer Rob opened the door to go out and walked smack into a horse, Stanley's horse. Stanley was beside it. We had only met him briefly once before. The night he visited, with his horse and his gun, he'd had a fight with his father and had to get away. We talked for awhile in the little shack, Stanley fondling his rifle the whole time. He'd been in Vietnam. It was bad. He slept with his rifle under the truck that night.

"Filthy disgusting hippies," he called us the next morning, laughing and drinking coffee as he watched us mix concrete and put the rocks into the walls of our root cellar. He helped clean the rocks with a wire brush.

Late in the fall Stanley's father came up the road with a friend, both of them very drunk. We were in the middle of our first season of hunters and didn't like it. The worst were the coon hunters who came at night, their dogs tearing through the woods all around us with their blood-curdling howls. It was a relief to recognize Hannibal, Stanley's father, with his long mane of gray hair. His friend Ben handed Rob his bottle of wine and collapsed onto his shoulder, saying, "I'm a good boy, ain't I, Rob? I'm a good boy, ain't I?" Stanley's father, drunk as he was, had a separate sense. He said to me, "Do you have your food laid in for the winter?"

At the town meeting in March, Stanley's father said to me, "Didn't see tracks for a few days up your road and got to wondering."

That spring his friend Ben put a bullet through his head. He was fifty-six. The next spring it was a thirty-three-year-old fellow. And after that it was the seventy-three-year-old dairy farmer who went out to the woods and covered up with alder brush first, so no one would find his body very soon. No one did.

• • •

By the way she talked about them and rode them alongside the highway all year long, you would think Stanley's sister Linda adored horses. She kept four of them in the barn out behind her father's place, though she had moved from there to a trailer down the road with her two-year-old daughter, Kim. Linda had pale, straw-blond hair and pale, scarred skin, and she was overweight in the sense of dumpy rather than of fat, so where her paleness, like her daughter's, might once have been the accompaniment to a lightness, instead she seemed now to drag, and be pasty, and to sink. Even on the back of a sleek, fast horse where she was happiest, she seemed to be dragging downward. Maybe it was because whoever she'd married at some pathetically young age was gone, or because she needed vitamins and fresh food. Maybe it was because she had taken up the fear of God, and it drained her. I didn't know what did it, I only knew the oomph had gone out of Linda long before.

And so she never cleaned the stables of her beloved horses and pretended not to see how stooped they had become as their own droppings pushed them up closer and closer to the ceiling. We had said we wanted manure for our gardens, and Linda offered us her barn. But when we started shoveling one early Saturday morning, a heap of it high on the truck hardly made a dent for the poor horses. It was demoralizing to shovel so long and to see how many more loads there really were. We were coated with flies and filth and just wanted to get out. But then the truck with all its load refused to start. Linda tried jumping it with cables but still it wouldn't go. We were only three miles from home, but it seemed as if we would be swallowed up by horseshit and never get there. And as we stood idly, swatting away the flies, Stanley came along. He had the same pasty pallor as Linda, but he was long-legged and wiry thin and his Adam's apple was like a yo-yo in his throat.

"Je-sus, wouldn't you know it," he said. "What d'ya need all *that* for?"

"Sssh," said Linda. "They cleaned it out, didn't they?"

Stanley found a heavy rope, attached it to an ancient, beat-up tractor, and somehow pulled the overloaded truck onto the road and up to the top of the first hill. From there we coasted down, building up more and more speed, a brown flurry spinning out behind us. But the motor never caught.

Stanley met us at the bottom of the hill. "Shit," was all he said.

He dragged us up to the top of the next steep hill. Again we coasted, faster and faster. Again the motor failed to make one little splutter.

"Wait a minute," Stanley said, as if he'd gotten an idea. But all he did was lean up against the tractor and light a cigarette, leaving us to block a whole lane of the road. You must have been able to smell us a good mile away, but Stanley could as easily have been standing in a field of new-cut hay, for all he seemed to notice the smell, or care.

Finally, without a word, he attached the rope again, hoisted himself back onto the seat, and pulled us to the top of the third and final hill.

"I'm gonna bust the goddamned tractor for your stupid load of shit," he yelled, unfastening the rope.

This time the motor caught.

Later that day, Stanley came by our gardens as we shoveled out the truck.

"You'd do a damn sight better with a sack of 10-10-10," he said, crushing a cigarette with the heel of his cowboy boot.

"Shut up and get yourself a beer," I told him. "Over in the ice chest."

He opened a beer, rolled up the sleeves of his plaid shirt, and squatted down on his haunches. He could squat like that for hours at a time, and with us, as we worked, he often did.

"I went over there to 'Nam," he said, taking a long swig. "I was out there putting my butt on the line for the American Way of Life." He swallowed another mouthful, then wiped his chin on his shoulder. "And you guys, you toss it back in my face." He chug-a-lugged the rest of the can, then crumpled it in one hand. We kept shoveling. He stood up. "It's Commies, you know, who fertilize with shit. Je-sus, the Chinks use their *own*." He spat off to one side. "Night soil, for Chrissakes."

Rob said, "Most of them don't have electricity, either."

"Damn right," said Stanley.

"Or eat meat," I added.

"So you admit it!" he bellowed. "You hippie Commie creeps! Christ! What the hell am I doing here?"

"That's a good question," said Rob.

Stanley went to the ice chest, got another beer, and squatted back down.

• • •

First you have to understand what I mean by road. I do not mean a length of path that goes from here to there, because even at its best season our road petered out before it ever got to *there*. Once, though, it had been the major stagecoach route between Atkinson and Pineland, more than three miles long, with thirteen houses and a school. In those days the road came the mile in to the Dinkins place—which eventually became our place, and would someday be someone else's, but which would remain forever the Dinkins place in the lore of the locals who might have long since forgotten who the Dinkins ever were—and passed on to other households, where crops were scratched from acid soil and children grew and the cycles of life repeated themselves grimly but adequately for several generations until no one could stand the grimness any more. Then, after rising up Howell Hill, skirting along the Howell family's fields, and descending steeply the other side, the road bridged a small but persistent river and proceeded directly into Pineland and the pulp mill. What is left of this poor road now makes the rise up to the Howell place and stops abruptly, only a dip in the tall grasses suggesting what might have been the last rutted efforts to continue toward the river, now unbridged.

But there is no point discussing the road at Howell Hill, because except for a few brief months each year you can only get as far as our place—the Dinkins place—by foot or ski. Because what I mean by road is now the most basic, elemental dirt: unadorned by paving or gravel or drainage, unmaintained for several decades, it now reverts during spring thaws and autumn torrents to a slimy, bottomless gick. The thirteen houses and the school long ago fell or burned, and only the Howell and the Dinkins places still have a semblance of fields and a spacing of ancient maples which clearly shape where once stood house and barn. The rest of the cellar holes have grown over with dense woods, and sunlight cannot get through these to the road. An ancient ditch alongside of it is the resting place for leaves, which have settled unhindered through decades of autumn, and brush tossed casually aside by those who cut logs for pulp or fire. And so moisture has had no place to go for years except deeper and deeper. It oozes down between rocks and clay, between sand and stones; it penetrates, saturates, and stays. A few sections of the road are like quicksand right into the middle of summer. By the beginning of June a four-wheel-drive truck might mush through, but then what you have is truly mush, ruts which no car can survive and no hand-held shovel can level. And so our ancient Power Wagon truck more often than not sat powerless atop the driveway—itself merely a strip of withered grasses molded into shallow ruts—until any car at all could have made it through.

"Nobody'll ever bother you way back there," chuckled Phyllis Bailey when we went to pay the excise tax on the vehicles.

"The Dinkins place!" said Arnold Perkins when we first bought a gallon of fresh milk. "Why who the hell would want to live all the way back there!"

That is what I mean by road.

Weeks went by without the sight of another person, weeks when the two of us were alone with the road and the land, which themselves became beings who lived and breathed. The utter quiet, too, had a soul all of its own. And the hillside which rose up steeply just across the road was as much a member of our household as Rob or me, a cranky old relation who'd moved in and needed to be reckoned with each day. It cut out the earliest hours of morning sunlight all year long. Down it slid the first fall frosts, which spared the upper elevations where no one ever tried to farm, and settled in a lethal blanket on our tomatoes, squash, and corn. It had a sense of mischief, this hill. In October it could disappear completely in a fog, masquerading as a grassy plain, until the fog lifted and it burst into a curtain of reds and oranges so triumphant that we could not help but forgive it the frosts and shadows.

And then, on the thin edge between two seasons, came the rains and winds, the whipping of air, the dense tumble of leaves: our world spun and shook itself out. A calm might follow, and if we were lucky this calm lasted a few days, the snows held off, and the motion of the earth then was the gentle rhythm of light and dark, freeze and thaw. Even the touch of cold on these days was a soothing touch. In the mornings the fields shimmered under frost. The few leaves that still hung from trees were faded and dried to a pallor so fragile as to be translucent. The sun played them like bells, only it was the chime of light and not a usual sound. These days just before winter the earth held its breath, and to live inside that breath was to live inside the most delicate web, the sheerest gauze of time, where music and light and touch were all the same.

• • •

I daydreamed in the outhouse, looking out through a clump of firs. I let my eyes make a lazy tour around the edges of the plywood subfloor a few yards away, delineating the space that would confine and shelter us, once walls and roof were done. I looked at the cornstalks withering in the garden, the piles of compost and mulch. I took in the glimmers of the last fall colors: a few orange leaves, a few golden apples, and behind them the pines, determined in their green. A plane passed overhead; I heard the drone, then it was gone. I sat in silence, looking out.

Suddenly there was a rustling of leaves too clumsy and loud to be a bird or a rabbit or a cat. My breath stopped. Heavy footsteps through the leaves got closer and closer. Directly in front of me, just a few feet away, then passing me quickly from left to right, then out of sight, was a hunter, swathed in bright new out-of-state orange. As he strode so briskly through the clearing he never looked around him, he never saw me, the creature crouching in the firs, he never detected the breath stopped in fear nor the eyes open wide fixed squarely upon him.

I thought: today, deer, you are safe.

• • •

We were trying to get one wall framed in before dark. A pickup truck stopped at the top of the driveway. We heard a door slam and waited for another, but there wasn't another.

"Just one, anyway," sighed Rob. He ran up the hill before whoever it was had a chance to come down. Days were short; we had no time for small talk. Rob disarmed people with his innocent, friendly manner; they didn't catch on until afterwards that he'd sent them away.

Often they were drunk when they came driving up this road.

He was just one man, this one, tall and swaggering but not drunk. Mean, though. He stood beside the bashed-up truck. "Whatcha doin' here?" he asked gruffly. "This is *my* place."

Rob laughed nervously. The guy snarled. "Well," said Rob. "We bought it fair and square six months ago, you can check at the registry of deeds."

"Shit!" said the guy. "Whoever sold it had no right. It's the Dinkins place."

Rob chuckled. "Old man Dinkins has been dead for twenty years."

"The old man was my grandfather. I'm Matt Dinkins, and I'm not dead."

"Well, whadya know, I'm glad to meet you," said Rob, smiling, and he reached out with his hand to shake.

"Christ," said Dinkins, untaken by Rob's amiable gesture. He kept his hands in his pockets. "The place is *mine* now."

"Hey," said Rob. "There've been a few owners since your grandfather had it, you know."

"Tough shit," growled the mean Dinkins. "Now that I'm back, it's mine."

"Where've you been?" asked Rob, hoping a little chitchat could still warm the fellow up.

"State Pen in Indiana, seven years."

"Huh," said Rob, trying to think what it was that called for seven years. In his mind went a procession of manslaughter, armed robbery, rape, and arson, but he didn't have a clue as to what they gave for what, let alone in Indiana.

"Huh yourself," said the mean Dinkins, getting back into his pickup. "You better clear offa here before the next time. I aim to move back." To make his point, he spit into the grass. Then he drove away.

Three days later we were at the little store at the intersection five miles away. Men were talking beside the old pot-bellied stove. We overheard one say the name Matt Dinkins. Rob joined the group and said, "Matt Dinkins? He came back and hassled us the other day."

All the men stopped talking and took stock of us. We could see it going through their heads: hippie couple, Dinkins place. Silent, their faces immobile, they each went through their private range of scorn and pity for us, taking in Rob's long hair and straggly beard, me without a bra.

"Ay-yup," said Freddie, owner of the store. "Well he won't be botherin' you no more."

"That's for sure," said a roly-poly little man in stiff denim overalls.

"He was botherin' his folks, you know, pushin' around his parents somethin' bad, or so she said," said Freddie.

"His sister, that is," explained the roly-poly man. "She's the one what gave it to him right in the back."

"In cold blood," said a tall thin game warden in dark glasses.

"With her father's .22," said the roly-poly man.

"I don't blame her none," said the game warden.

I felt my jaw drop. Rob said, "Whew!" turning red with mixed emotions. It must have seemed to them that he'd go on with more, so they all waited. But he couldn't muster any words.

The roly-poly man looked up into his face and shook his head. "Christ, young fella, nobody'll go botherin' you folks all the way back there."

• • •

We walked up the road with knapsacks of groceries on our backs. The sinkholes of mud were hidden by matted leaves. Every few paces our boots got sucked in, right up to the ankles, and the suction pops of our steps were the only sounds we heard, except for crows flapping and cawing overhead. There were horse hoof tracks in the mud, and then they trailed off where the horses must have been taken to more solid ground. Mesmerized by the rhythm of our own slithery footsteps, we forgot about horses. But just before the house site we noticed what appeared to be long, rectangular leaves hanging from the twigs of a straggly birch sapling. We drew closer and saw they were pieces of paper, signs of human life not ours. First hesitating, then impatient, Rob grabbed one, unfolded it, sighed, and handed it to me. It was the *Watchtower* of the Jehovah's Witnesses.

2. Builders

SHELDON AND PATTY MOVED UP from Connecticut with their trust fund onto the property across from Stanley and his father's. They planned to build a stone house and the best possible farm; Sheldon made sure he had everything before he began. He bought a four-wheel-drive jeep, a cement-mixer, a tractor, a dump truck, a work horse, a small bulldozer, and a welding unit. He got a good deal on all of them. None of them worked. He was planning to fix them.

Patty produced cheeses, sourdough breads, and sprouts. She pumped the family with fresh vegetables, wheat germ, brewer's yeast, and homemade yogurt. But she was overweight. Sheldon had high blood pressure. One child was hyperactive, the other was anorexic. Something was wrong.

Patty took up gossiping and told stories of other people's domestic failures, their marriages breaking up, their children running wild, their overuse of refined sugars. She avoided people who were happy, whose gardens thrived, whose children were well behaved, who had finished building their houses. She took up ceramics and went religiously to class twice a week. She made ceramic toothbrush holders, soup bowls with the family names, a ceramic model of the unbuilt house, a ceramic pie with four and twenty blackbirds popping out of it, and ceramic cheeses—hunks of Gouda, Emmenthaler, Camembert, bleu, even a perfect pale orange replica of aged Canadian cheddar.

Each year Sheldon laid down the floor and completed one course of stonework on the house. Each fall he tore up the floor so it would not get spoiled in the winter weather. One winter the cellar heaved and Sheldon had to start two walls over again. He would not let Patty work on the house because he knew she'd do it wrong. For the time being they lived in two burned-out rooms of the wrecked house that had been on the land when they bought it. They all slept in the same cold, drafty room. One time Patty and the kids left for three days so Sheldon could put in some insulation, but instead he read *Reader's Digest* condensations. When Patty hired someone to finish the insulation and put up shelves, Sheldon went into a rage.

They sold the horse and got a six-by-six truck. Patty took up with the Mormons. Sheldon was certain that when the world collapsed and they were the only ones ready, the marauding hordes of stupid and unprepared people would come and try to get their stuff, so he bought a rifle and a pistol, just in case.

Patty got pregnant. She had a baby.

• • •

It happened not just once but twice. Katie and David salvaged the lumber from a house which had to be destroyed. They hauled it, truckload by truckload, up the two miles of deeply rutted woods road to the site where they planned to build, on the acres they had bought with the money David earned digging clams, after he'd stopped teaching English. And the lumber was stolen, every weathered board and hand-hewn beam and worm-infested two-by-four. Twice. First one winter, then the next. Two years, two houses, two dreams gone. The third year they moved themselves with the lumber to the top of the hill, to guard it and build with it through the winter. Like us, they lived in a little shack while they built, but they lived there through most of one entire year and with Matthew and Heather, their children.

In the winter nights the fire in the small stove burned out or blew out from the draft. The dog's water froze. The condensation from four people breathing in such a small space froze. And every night little Matthew, who slept under mountains of blankets in one corner, was glued by his hair with frozen condensation to the wall. Every morning Katie started out by peeling Matthew off the wall.

Still, they began to build a house. Two stories, post and beam. By summer when it came time to get the walls into the air, they tried doing the job themselves with the truck and block-and-tackle, but it was just too enormous a task. So when the road dried out they had a house-raising party and we came to help from all our little hideouts in the woods, some of us in our big clunky trucks, some in cars which had to be left at the bottom of the hill. Couples and small children, dogs, babies, we formed a procession up that road, following the outer edges of the ruts by truck or foot, bearing bean casseroles and whole grain breads, rhubarb cobblers and a dozen fresh-picked salads. And then we lined up alongside the framed walls, each of us braced to lift, and at David's calm and quiet call, "One, two, three, *up!*" the walls arose. It took no great power, it simply took two hundred fingertips in unison. And there it was: the frame of a house standing where nothing had stood just an hour before. The dogs barked, the children romped, the babies gurgled, and we feasted in celebration of our work.

Katie planted flowers all around the house that summer. She toasted cheese sandwiches on the top of the woodstove. She got permission to teach the kids at home and in the fall she gave lessons in history, English, and art. Her teeth came loose and traveled in her gums, and David, finding no work nearby, slogged out at some ungodly hour to catch the clams abandoned by a tide sixty miles away. The dog ran down the hill and bit the neighbor's daughter. He had to be destroyed. They bought a pony which hauled water, gave the children rides, and ate up all the garden.

Once, during a fight, when Katie was dissatisfied again just when she had everything she thought she ever wanted, David picked up the brand new chainsaw and applied it to a cedar post holding up the house. She was too stunned to try to stop him. He did manage to stop himself before he got halfway through the post, before he moved on to any others. But that first deep gash was there forever after.

Matthew and Heather asked to go to school the second year. They agreed to walk down the hill, to catch the bus on time, to walk back up the hill at night, no matter what. And they did. They never missed a day.

• • •

Genie and Jeff lived in an old chicken coop. It was okay. They'd once lived at the top of a sixth-floor walk-up all the way east on East Second Street while Jeff, stuck for years in the math department at CCNY, tried to write a dissertation on infinity. Their neighbors further down on unpaved Tuttle Road lived in a chicken coop too, but theirs wasn't so okay. The neighbors had always lived in theirs and probably always would. Now it was surrounded on all sides by carcasses of cars and trucks all oxidized to the same deep burnt sienna, metals originating in different generations now uniformly flaking into layers like fine rust phylo pastry. Around Genie and Jeff's chicken coop, by contrast, was lumber: sweet-smelling newly milled boards and two-by-fours, weathered gray timbers salvaged from noble barns, intricately carved old doors, bales of shingles, a couple of mahogany church pews sitting upright and reverent beside the herb garden. Genie and Jeff were building a dome, or at least they were getting ready to. Some of the older stuff had been piled up there for two or three years. But they didn't seem to mind the coop: it was warm, it was cozy, and by our first summer they'd already had two children there. Anyway, they weren't really *living* in a chicken coop; eventually they'd be in the dome to live for real. But no rush. Upward mobility was no longer their thing. Their kid played with the neighbors' kids, Jeff tinkered with the neighbors on their temperamental engines. Everybody got along. For the time being, the chicken coop was sort of fun. A goof. The neighbors, though, really lived in theirs. *That* was depressing.

Early on, Genie and Jeff had put in four thermopane windows, two that even opened, and generous rolls of insulation, too: you'd duck through the door and enter a long squat box lined with tinfoil. Jeff, who'd be huge anywhere, couldn't stand up straight in his house, and whenever he stood up too fast his head got caught in fiberglass. Then, if he sat down too hard on the armchair with the broken springs, his bottom hit the floor. The up and down of this house were both out to get him, but he was mellow and uncomplaining. He'd light another joint. Someday soon, in the dome, he'd stand up straight. "I'll be playing basketball in the dome someday!" he boasted once.

Genie was petite, a sturdy woman but tiny: she could walk through the door without ducking, and the ceiling didn't so much as graze the top of her head when she stood up. But I almost never saw her standing. Every time we went there our first summer, she was sitting on the old couch, serene and smiling, nursing the new baby or, sometimes, still, the two year old, her long blond hair falling straight to her waist, her long skirt billowing around her ankles. On a shelf all along one tinfoil wall were the big jars of her herbal potions, cloudy liquids of strange fermenting greens and yellows. Occasional bubbles drifted upward through the murkiness. Sometimes I wondered what was really brewing in there. The baby never cried.

Genie and Jeff had electricity. They had TV. They were the only ones of us who did. So every few days that first summer we'd drive out our road and then four or five miles along the highway and up Tuttle Road to the chicken coop to watch Watergate. Others would come there, too. We'd scrunch up together on the floor while Genie and Jeff sat regally in their usual places. One day in June, John Dean's head filled up the screen.

"Look at him sweat," Jeff chortled.

"No, that's just the glare from the TV lights," countered Genie.

"Another receding hairline. They've all got 'em," I added. "All these men."

Katie giggled. "All these big foreheads. Big sweaty Republican foreheads." Our men of course had youthful full heads of hair and then some, David's gathered back in a bushy mass, Rob's in a long ponytail down his back, Jeff's hanging loose to his shoulders.

"It's what happens when you lie and cheat and steal. You lose your hair," said David.

Rob chimed in. "Like George Mitchell."

"Ugh." Genie shuddered, shifting the baby to the other breast. "That pasty-faced jerk. Mitchell was the model for Mr. Potatohead. Didja know that?"

"That's an insult to the Maine potato," I said.

"To potatoes everywhere," said Rob.

"Okay, the styrofoam kind."

"Remember that?" mused Rob. "You pinned the eyebrows on. The ears. The nose."

Jeff drew on a joint, then passed it to Rob. "And Haldeman."

"Uh-uh, he's got his hair. It's Ehrlichman who's going bald," Genie corrected.

"Whichever. I can't keep them straight."

"Rosencrantz and Guildenstern," said David. "Haldeman and Ehrlichman. They're all the same."

Our silly banter went round and round, the joint went round and round. How long had it been since any of us had taken the government, the men in power and their thinning hair (cut short) with anything more than a grain of salt? They'd lost us years ago with their stock markets and processed foods and ticky tacky houses, their America-love-it-or-leave-it, their vicious contempt for the poor and black and foreign. But most of all what turned us away and made them past redemption was their war, the bombing they kept going even now, though American troops were finally out.

Then words we actually *heard* emanated from the screen, from the mouth under the sweaty forehead off which the light bounced in a scrubbed-boy gleam:

"There was a cancer growing on the presidency, and if the cancer was not removed, the president himself would be killed by it."

"Huh?"

"Who does he say said that to *who?*"

"Yahoo!" yelped Jeff. "Let that cancer run its course!"

"Shut up now," said Genie.

"Dean says that's what *he* told *Nixon.*"

We hushed ourselves. The circuit of the joint stopped still. We listened. Dean had warned him: they would have to cut the cancer out to save this presidency's life. And so the dirty tricks, the cover-up, the president's complicity, would all turn out to be real and true, here Nixon's own one-time legal mind just said so. If *he* could be believed.

Katie said, "This gang of hooligans, they planned it from the start, right in the White House."

"Wow."

"No shit."

"A coup."

We were impressed. Right there on TV the scummy, cheating underbelly of the guys in charge began to bare itself. Beyond even our own wildest condemnations, there it was. We would not have put anything past them, but we hadn't yet figured on all *this*.

Genie unhooked the sleeping baby from her left breast and passed him to Jeff. The two-year-old scrambled up on her lap. Genie guided her to the right nipple.

"Far out," she said. "Finally, good daytime TV."

"We can't miss this now, can we?" said Jeff, patting the baby on his shoulder.

"You'll just have to slow down on the dome," chuckled Genie. "Spend more time watching."

"Fuck it," said Jeff. "This is history. How often do we get to see a president come toppling down? You're right, I'll just have to slow down on the dome."

• • •

"This house is a *fortress!*" exclaimed DeeDee, standing in the middle of the large room with her legs apart, braced as if a hurricane were blowing through. She was eight months pregnant and had her flannel shirt tied in a knot over the taut round bulge that was the baby. Her hair fell in a cascade of sun-streaked ripples down her back, almost to her waist. It was November, but her face was still weathered and tanned to an indelible ruddy brown.

"The posts underneath are concrete," she said. "The walls are all six inches thick. There's six inches of insulation all around and twelve inches in the ceiling."

We followed her. She hung several long braided strands of enormous red onions on a wall already laden with garlic and drying herbs. She quickly lined up pumpkins and orange hubbard squash on a counter in the sun. The whole front of the house was windows. We waited while she dashed out and brought in a bushel of carrots layered in sand. Through a trap door in the floor she lowered them into the root cellar.

"Come look," she commanded, and we followed her down the ladder into the cellar, ducking underneath the cabbages that hung from the low ceiling.

"We *built* all this," she said. "Every stone came from the garden."

We could barely see the stonework because the deep wooden shelves built along all four walls bulged with carefully packed crates of turnips, beets, carrots, and apples.

"They last until *April* down here!" she announced.

Then she led us back out to the garden, which was where she and Walter truly lived; the fortress was simply a place where they stored and cooked and ate what flourished from the garden, where they rested and washed from their work in the garden, where they planned each year's garden on graph paper in the depths of February nights.

"We use *no* power tools," DeeDee proclaimed. "We are completely independent." And a few years later, when her parents gifted them with a windmill, they used it only for hauling water up from a well to feed the garden and never to put so much as a light bulb inside the house.

"We have *nothing* to do with American capitalism, with its waste and its poisons." She began shoveling a rich, black, loamy compost into the wheelbarrow, then rolled it quickly down a garden row, past brussels sprouts plants that came up to our thighs. We followed her to the end of the garden and into the orchard. She got on her knees and began to place handfuls of compost in careful circles around the base of a young apple tree. "Our children will be free. They won't be poisoned. Not their bodies, not their minds." She moved on to the next tree. Walter came along with a cartful of straw mulch, which he applied directly over DeeDee's compost. Though his muscles bulged he was spindly and thin, and his thick glasses made him look like the school teacher he used to be.

"Our life is whole," he said, smiling. "What's right for it will fit. It's like one piece, you know what I mean?" He smiled again. I didn't know what he meant, but I smiled back. "Even children won't change our lives," he said.

Then they finished up the compost, went into the house, and lit a joint.

"This baby will *not* change our lives," said DeeDee, three weeks later. She still held onto a pile of mulch as she lay down on the garden path, clutching her belly. We had a stopwatch and timed the contractions. They were close. The doctor who'd agreed to do the delivery at home was napping in the house.

"We should wake up Tom," I said.

"No," said DeeDee. "It's not time yet."

She got up and began to spread the straw around the brussels sprouts plants. She finished one row, lay down, endured a contraction, and started the next row.

"It may be *days* before I have another chance to finish this," she said. "They're predicting so much rain."

Rob put the stopwatch back into his pocket. We could hear Walter pounding on the other side of the house, where he was shingling the new summer kitchen. Even after DeeDee came in, washed up, woke the doctor, and howled with fast contractions, Walter was out hammering on the summer kitchen wall.

"Should I come in now?" he hollered down from the ladder.

"*Not yet!*" shrieked DeeDee. A contraction sneaked up on her and she gasped. The breathing techniques we'd all learned were of no use to her. She leaned back against the wall, sweat streaming down her face and neck. I wiped her face with a damp cloth and she smiled at me like an angel. If she was afraid she did not let on; and if the doctor was, neither did he. The pounding on the summer kitchen wall reassured them both that things were normal.

Rob massaged DeeDee's belly. I timed the contractions, but there was no rhythm to them anymore.

"The pains are so irregular," I said.

DeeDee suddenly sat up straight. "*Not pains!*" she yelled. "They are *not* pains, Sonia! They're *contractions*. There is *no* comparison!" Then, wincing, she leaned back and howled.

Then the changes happened very fast. I grabbed the flashlight and aimed it on the crowning head. The doctor had to make a cut but DeeDee didn't care. A little bit more of the head made an appearance, then more, then what seemed like a vast amount of hair.

"*Come—out—baby!*" screamed DeeDee.

In two more seconds, the little baby girl with the full head of dark brown hair was out.

Walter went to the garden to bury the placenta. DeeDee would not use a chamber pot, but stumbled out the door and squatted just in front. The doctor bathed the baby with warm water from the kettle. DeeDee returned and lay down with the infant sprawled on her chest, and she smiled again, a tender, tired smile, a glow added to the soft kerosene light. "My baby," she murmured. "My love. My house." She smiled more and closed her eyes. "We are a fortress," she said in a whisper. Then she fell asleep.

• • •

"This house should be a fortress," said Rob as he unloaded a stack of two-by-fours from the truck.

"Who says?" I asked.

He stopped with the lumber poised in mid-air. "What do you mean, 'who says'? Anybody knows that."

"I don't," I said. "I just want someplace to live."

He lowered the two-by-fours and arranged them on the pile. "Well I want someplace that will last forever."

"A mausoleum," I said.

"No, a house," he replied.

And that was our first fight in the woods.

Later he said, "The foundation is everything. If we can't afford a full cellar, which we can't, then concrete posts are the next best thing."

"Okay," I said.

"Because they'll *endure*," he added.

"All *right*," I snapped.

He read all the authorities on mixing concrete, copying recipes into a notebook. He found the gravel pits with the most even-sized gravel, a source of the cleanest sand. A backhoe came and dug out sixteen holes each eight feet deep, and we spent a week full of strings, plumbs and levels, setting in the sturdy forms we'd bought. When they were all perfectly upright and aligned, we borrowed a cement mixer, measured our ingredients, mixed batches of concrete to the ideal consistency, and poured. How slowly, how laboriously, how painstakingly we made those sixteen posts. And finally they were there, in four perfectly straight rows. We backfilled around them, we let them cure.

Then we set the first beam on the first row of posts, and the front of the house suddenly appeared: a line, a shape, a reality. Excited, Rob leaned the first two-by-four on the beam and whizzed through with the brand-new handsaw.

"Does this feel great!" he exclaimed. *Zip-zip-zip* went the saw, and the end of the two-by-four dropped neatly off, hitting the ground with a light clunk. But then we heard a pop, too. And a plop. A concrete post fell over, sheered off at ground level.

"Oh God, *no!*"

Inside, the post looked wet, the texture was uneven. Was it punky concrete, or hadn't it cured? We didn't know.

"Well," I said. "We'll have to replace that one."

Rob was silent for a several moments. "How do you know it's just *one?*" he shouted then. He raised his foot, and with a motion none too strenuous he kicked over a second post.

"There," he said flatly.

Stanley came with a winch and helped us pull the posts out of the ground, all sixteen. He helped us cut down sixteen sturdy cedars. We peeled the bark off each of them with a drawknife, filling the site with snakes of coarse cedar. We shoved a post into each hole and leveled them all with a chainsaw the best we could.

"Shit," said Rob. Unlike me, I began to understand, he'd had a dream, a precise idea of what we were doing here. Now he had a disappointment. *"These* won't last forever."

I bit my lip.

Stanley burst out with a loud guffaw. "Christ," he said. "Neither will *you.*"

• • •

To rebuild a cellar wall that had caved in, Sheldon and Patty needed to remove dozens of cubic yards of soil from all around it. When most of the summer went by and they still hadn't dug it out, they began to panic. They thought of the house-raising party that had worked so nicely for Katie and David and decided there would be no better way to clear their wall than with a work party. So they invited us all to bring a shovel and a dish for a potluck supper, and good sports that we were, we all emerged again from our little clearings in the woods, even Stanley and his father from across the road.

Shoveling was no house-raising. It may have been a job divided by twenty people, but in the end it was just you and your shovel, or maybe you and a wheelbarrow, and it was labor, hot and hard. Nobody talked. We shoveled for an hour, then we shoveled for another hour, and in the middle of the third hour Stanley said, "How about some beer and grub now?"

Sheldon's little black goatee barely moved when he frowned. Patty dug her shovel deep into a pile of packed clay, as if to set a good example, and said, "Oh, c'mon now, let's finish up!"

Stanley's father, Hannibal, worked next to me. He mumbled loudly, "Had an easier time digging trenches in the war." He put down his shovel and sat on a large rock.

Sheldon frowned at him. Hannibal frowned right back and lit a cigarette.

Stanley dug in harder with his shovel, anger had him all fired up, and when he finished digging out the end where he had started, he moved along helping all the rest of us, like some human backhoe gone berserk. You could see each of his arm muscles tighten as they were called to action, and his T-shirt was drenched in sweat. We couldn't slow him down. The job must have finished an hour sooner, thanks to Stanley.

"Christ," said Hannibal, "he'd be good on a chain gang."

Stanley took his T-shirt off and lit a cigarette.

Patty said, "There! Now you can have something to eat."

Stanley stood face to face with her. She had a horsey build and was nearly as tall as he was. She grinned contentedly.

"No thank you!" he shouted, spitting out the words, and he stomped away in the direction of his father's house.

• • •

Although we had built the little shack planning to have the house finished by October, the second set of posts weren't even in the ground until mid-November, when winter set in, too. We built a little woodshed onto the little shack, borrowed a small stove, and arose more and more times in the night to stoke it. The cat and dog dug their way under the blankets. The snows started. The winds howled. There was half an inch of pressed cardboard between the elements and us, between what had suddenly become subzero tundra and 840 cubic feet of warmed air.

We braved the weather and we built, not because we were brave but because we had nowhere else to go, and eventually the words in the books we read to learn how to build became entities of space brought into meaning by two-by-fours: floor joists, subfloor, sills; the frame appeared. Most nights there was a snowfall or a wind squall. Nearly every morning we started work by shoveling out the house. Then, while Rob pounded boards onto the frame, I peeled ice off each new board with the drawknife. Slivers and shavings of ice fell at my feet. Nails sprung out of the frozen boards. Rob swore, pounded, cut. Every few hours I ran into the shack, stoked the stove, strung out the latest pairs of frozen gloves above it, pet the lumps in the quilt that were the cat and dog, and ran back out. And with this routine the house closed in, little by little it became walls, windows, roof, floor. We moved a stove in and watched the ice shavings melt. We unfurled rolls of fiberglass and stuffed the walls with insulation, then we covered up the insulation with more thawing boards. And one day late in January when the sky was a threatening gray, just before the next heavy snow, we moved in.

Stanley watched us unpack boxes.

"Books," he said, disgusted. "Don'tcha have anything but books in there?"

We lined them up neatly on the clean pine shelves.

"Je-sus H. Christ," he muttered, stomping out a cigarette on the brand new floor. I felt a protest rise in my throat. I swallowed it. "Goddamn hippie longhair Commie bookworms."

• • •

Two weeks later came the deepest dip below zero, the fiercest wind. It was still warm in the house and the Ashley stove was humming right along, stoked for a good eight hours more, but little puffs of cold had begun to seep in around the windows. This was the test: had we built a true shelter? We lit the cookstove, too, just to be safe, filling the whole box with maple and ash, woods that would burn hot and long. It was the first time we had lit both stoves together.

Suddenly it became eighty degrees in the house, then, very quickly, eight-five. And then ninety. We listened to the wind screaming and the popping of the trees as they froze through and through: *thwip!* Then *thwop!* And we were sweating. Ninety-five degrees, the stoves damped down as far as they could be, and all that slow-hot burning maple and ash were just getting started. We peeled off layers of clothing until we were stripped down to sweat and skin. And still it was too hot. We opened one window, then another, and finally we opened up a door. We lay on the bed and listened to the angry sound of pine needles whipping against the house and a shrillness in the wind that seemed to come from the innermost soul of cold. Another *thwip!* Another *thwop!* We heard the trees scream out. Then, dopey with heat, we fell asleep.

Hours later, it must have been the door banging back and forth in the wind that woke us, or the whistle of wind blowing across us through the room. And we found ourselves shivering, sprawled naked on the bed, with the fires both down to embers, a small snow drift in the doorway, and ice crusted thick on the windowsills.

3. Dog and Bunny Rabbit Stories

First you have to understand what I mean by dog. I do not mean a big furry mutt who knocks you over in a greeting, or a high-strung pedigree, or a robust watchdog who howls a threat with every foreign noise. Nor do I mean a poodle, malamute, sheepdog, setter, or anything you've learned to recognize or respect.

What I mean by dog is the runt of a litter who never grew, a black-and-white, short-haired, floppy-eared mix of Border collie, spaniel, and God knows what, with a tail that never stopped wagging. This was a lapdog who, at the sound of the word "Go," would run to the car and whine so expectantly and so insistently that we began to spell the word; an undersized beast who learned very quickly what "g-o" spelled; a ridiculous animal who, with her muzzle, tossed each pellet of dog food across the room in a one-dog game of pitch and catch before she would deign to eat it. This was Wiggle, our dog for all the years.

Stanley looked down at Wiggle, who was yipping at his toes, then at me. "Shit," he said. "You ought to get yourselves a *dog* someday."

That is what I mean by dog.

• • •

"Okay, Wiggle, go get that rabbit!" I pointed to the creature at the far side of the garden who was nibbling on my lettuce. "Go get it!"

Wiggle stood there wagging her tail. She looked up at me, then she looked at the rabbit, then she ran a few steps in place. She looked up at me again.

"Go get that rabbit, Wiggle." I wondered if I should spell it.

Wiggle finally made up her mind. She would get it. But she had learned so well *not* to run through the garden that instead of tearing off in one straight line across the lettuce rows, she ran along the periphery of the whole garden—up one side, along the end, and down the far side. And by the time she got there the rabbit had ruined three heads of lettuce and disappeared.

• • •

I sat on the back step in the early evening, after Rob had gone to work. This was during his stint as projectionist at the drive-in. It was sunset time. Quiet time. Not-yet-too-many-bugs time. The hills in the distance had turned purple-blue, and a light coating of sunset gold glinted on the garden. A gentle breeze rippled in the grasses, which were beginning to grow high around the house. It was very, very quiet. Wiggle lay beside me. And a rabbit hopped along and stopped, six feet away from us, and stared into my face. Wiggle lay there, wagged her tail twice, then closed her eyes. The rabbit hopped away.

• • •

Rob went to work. I watched the garden. It was dusk. Time for rabbits. And it did not take long: I saw the rabbit run into the lettuce patch. This time I knew what I was going to do: I was not going to wait for the dog. I was going to kill the rabbit myself. I had Millard Worlsley's pellet rifle and a lesson in how to use it. I grabbed it and quietly left the house, tiptoeing across the garden. "Annie Oak-ley," I sang to myself, the words from a record I owned twenty years before suddenly springing to memory to give me courage:

> "Tell us truly to our faces
> Is it true that you can shoot
> All the buttons right off a cowboy's suit
> And you do it at eleven hundred paces?"

I stalked over to the rabbit and got five feet from it. It stopped eating; half a lettuce leaf hung from its mouth. It was paralyzed, gazing straight at me. I poised the rifle on my shoulder.

> "There never was a gal
> Like Annie Oak-ley!"

I looked through the sighting. The rabbit gazed back up the barrel at me. Okay, rabbit, I said to myself: It's time to meet your maker. I pulled the trigger, bracing myself. But the gun didn't fire. I did it again. Again it didn't fire. I checked the rifle to make sure I had released all I was supposed to release and loaded all I was supposed to load. Everything was correct. The rabbit sat there, waiting patiently. I captured it through the lens again. It twitched its whiskers. The leaf still hung from its mouth. Black-seeded Simpson, slow to bolt. Okay, rabbit, meet your maker. "Bam!" I said. But the gun failed to fire. The rabbit, startled by the sound of my voice, dropped the lettuce leaf. I realized I could more easily have taken one step forward, picked up the rabbit, and strangled it with my bare hands.

"Okay, rabbit," I said. "Beat it!" The rabbit turned on its haunches and ran.

"There," I said.

I unloaded the rifle and went back into the house. Wiggle was lying in the armchair. She opened her eyes, looked at me adoringly, and wagged her tail. Then she went back to sleep.

4. *Lovers*

I WATCHED OUT THE KITCHEN WINdow as Rob climbed up the hill from the well. He struggled against the weight of two five-gallon buckets of water, one hanging from each hand. It was noon, the sky eerily dark: a solid bank of blue-gray cloud slumbered on the distant silhouette of blue-gray hills. While the cloud mass rested, it replenished; when it moved again, it would dump snow again. Rob's black watch cap fell partway down his eyes. Each of his steps was unnaturally slow: his tall rubber boots sank deep into the snow. He labored with the lifting of each foot up out of the snow to make the next step forward, back down into the snow and, at the same time, up the hill. His beard was white with hoarfrost. Loping along in his footsteps, Wiggle bounded breathlessly from one depression to the next, then missed, sank into a puff of untrampled white, and disappeared.

On the cookstove, a big kettle began to hum as it came to a boil. I moved it to the back burner, moved another kettle to the front. A third kettle rattled and sputtered on the Ashley stove, sending out a steady plume of steam. I tumbled an armful of more wood into both stoves.

When I opened the door, Wiggle slid in first, a wild cluster of ice balls stuck like barnacles to her snout, ice balls hanging so heavily from her underbelly that they brushed along the floor, ice balls swelling every toe. I pulled off as many as I could before she yelped and hid behind the stove, where she started to melt, biting ice from her paws. Rob set the buckets down in their place under the counter beside the sink.

"Enough?" he asked.

"Definitely," I said. "You first?"

"No, you." Condensation dripped from his beard. Off came his soggy ragg wool mittens, which I fit onto the metal drying rods at either side of the stove. Off came the big red down parka, which he hung on a peg. He sat on the bench and pulled at each boot, exposing dank socks fringed with snow.

I'd already positioned the metal tub close to the Ashley, and beside it two buckets Rob had brought up the day before, the chill now gone. We were prepared. Bath day. The house was steamy warm, but little currents of the icy outdoors scurried like mice along the floor, making it not so easy to undress. While I peeled off my layers of shirts and pants and thermals and socks, Rob poured in one kettle of boiling water, then another. Carefully he poured in part of a bucket, tested with a finger, poured in more. I stuck in my toe.

"Too hot still."

He let flow the rest of the bucket, profligately undoing his own hard work, the weight hauled up the hill.

I knew it was better to enter that water while it seemed too hot, because in not so very long it would seem too cold. I got both feet in, crouched, slowly lowered my bottom. Before I even touched, heat rose up to meet me. Then I was in. My thighs turned red. I clutched my knees, adjusting to the temperature before I let my arms down into the water or splashed it on my face. "Yikes, that's hot!" I screamed. And hooted with laughter. Wiggle jumped up, vigilant, growling at whatever made me scream. Then she settled down again, eyeing us skeptically, nose perched on wet paws. Now all was quiet except for the wind bellowing in the chimney and the splashes I made with soap and water.

Rob knelt behind me, submerged a washcloth, then began to scrub my back as I leaned forward to tackle first one callused foot, lopped over the opposite knee, then the other. The cloth was warm but rough on my shoulders, abrasive on my neck. Cleaning me was more woods work for him; he lit into it as he might to felling a tree or clearing a ditch, with all his unstinting energy. I was thoroughly scrubbed behind my ears, around my neck, under my arms.

Then his touch changed. Scrub turned into massage, massage into caress: he rubbed the small of my back with his palms, brought both hands around from behind, explored lightly under my breasts, then cupped them as he lathered them slowly, carefully, each one firming to his touch. He squeezed warm water from the cloth onto my nipples, he dipped it back into the tub and trickled out the water teasingly again, then he maneuvered to kneel beside me and took one nipple in his mouth. I lay back, resting my neck on the metal rim of the tub. And while he sucked, soapy water bubbling into his moustache and beard, his hand and the washcloth worked their way down from my breasts to my belly. He circled round and round with his weather-worn fingers, those wood-chopping, potato-picking, fish-gutting fingers, along my stomach, then down. And as those fingers might probe at berries in harvest or the small parts of temperamental tools to fix, they probed and caressed and cleaned me until I cried out.

Wiggle leapt up alarmed again, growling again. Rob pushed himself away from me, away from the tub, and stood. I leapt up to my own feet, dripping wet, and Rob wrapped me quickly in a big towel and rubbed me all over until I was almost dry. Leaving the full tub of lukewarm water in the middle of the kitchen floor, we rushed to bed.

• • •

I was weeding around a vigorous two-inch growth of new pea vines, thinning out the wispiest of carrot tops. The two early-planted vegetables alternated companionably in rows. The sun was warm, the air was warm, the temperature absolutely right on my skin and all around me. It was suddenly crystal clear: I belonged. I belonged here. Everything here belonged here. Existence made the utmost sense. Well-being purred in my chest, cradled every nerve. I pulled weeds. The work had its own logic, its own momentum, and I melted into it with barely a thought, lulled by the distant hum of insects and the full deep smell of sunlight-heated soil that gently prickled in my nostrils. I crouched when my muscles could take it, scooted along each row on my knees or bottom when they couldn't. As I disentangled minuscule root hairs of July's Royal Chantenays and August's Scarlet Nantes, earthworms looped out of fingers' way. Blackflies didn't much bother me; I was coated with some herbal stuff, pennyroyal-based, and I blew at the flies when they got too near my face. No anxiety disrupted my ease, no old rancors, puzzles, doubts, or dreads intruded. I was just here. I was just part of the scene; if I'd had a tail I would have swished it.

Rob came along with a wheelbarrow of soft loamy mulch. He started to spread it lightly between the rows I'd already done, off at the far end of the smaller patch. He tossed a shovelful at careful intervals, then went back with a rake to scratch it in the soil. Our routine was silent. Every so often he smiled. I smiled.

I stood up. There was a fullness in my body that wanted out, an amplitude pushing beyond the borders of my skin. I unbuttoned my denim shirt and took it off. Rob stopped raking. I felt his gaze and the gaze of the sun and the warm ripples of breeze on my breasts. I knelt back down and finished out my row of carrots, tweaking out the surplus of little plants, leaving one or two every inch along. I stood again. Rob kept shoveling but had one eye on me. I kicked off my left boot, then the right. I pulled off my socks. I stood for a minute, hearing the hum and thrum of the gentle insect life around us. Then I stepped out of my jeans. In my panties, I crouched down to start weeding the next row of peas. Rob shoveled, Rob raked.

Halfway along the row, my muscles straining badly from the crouch, I stood up again. Rob watched. I rolled my panties down my legs and kicked them off. He looked me up and down: no new sight, but an unusual backdrop, an unusual time. He smiled. He changed the shovel for the rake and began to spread the compost evenly beside the row of accordion-leafed baby chard.

I tiptoed through the rows and moved behind him. While he still worked, I pressed against him, let my own body's moves double up with his: chest pressed to back, arm over arm, leg nestled inside leg, I bent and pushed and pulled with him, guiding the rake. He was hot, his shirt was damp, I was swallowed up in his pungency of sweat and wet flannel and compost and pennyroyal and sun. I reached around and loosened up his shirt, stroked the coarse hairs at his navel. He stepped forward with one foot: in this semi-stride, my knee hugged the back of his thigh. After we held there for awhile, my weight easing onto his, he quickly turned around. Now we were face to face. Soon we were on the grass. Then we were entwined.

The next day we were so swollen and aflame with blackfly bites that neither of us could dress. We couldn't work. We couldn't sleep or lie flat or even sit. All we could do was burn and itch and sting and ache. We could not bear each other's touch as we slathered aloe on our welt-erupted backs. We snapped, we snarled, imprisoned in our nest, with nothing but the two of us, our bodies and our pain.

Oh love, oh springtime, oh one-ness with the universe!

• • •

It was a long day and a hot and humid day, again that first summer, and we went with DeeDee and Walter to a salvage yard many miles away in Ellsworth, where they sometimes got old doors and windows and we might, someday, too. They scrutinized, they hemmed and hawed, they had a languid conversation with the owner, long silences interrupted mostly by toneless grunts. Walter circled around the shards of dismembered houses, shaky piles of wormy lumber, knobs and bolts and metal fixtures jumbled in rusty heaps. He tugged at his ragged beard, kicked his heel into the dirt like a moody horse. DeeDee swabbed sweat from her forehead now and then, squinted at me and grinned. As usual her plaid shirt was tied above the bare bulge of her pregnant belly. Eventually, somehow they settled on an item and a price, and roped a carved oak door atop their beat-up old white van. So it was a work day, for them who always worked, but it was a stifling hot day, and on the way home they drove to a lake tucked into the woods off an unmarked road.

DeeDee jumped from the vehicle first and ran to a rock jutting into the water. In a few quick movements she untied and pulled off all her clothes. With her long frizzy hair rippling down her back, she turned slowly toward us and grinned. Her heavy breasts were amazingly erect, her belly protruded in a perfect semi-circle. The last bright rays of the setting sun sprayed toward us through the trees behind her silhouette, outlining her fecundity in gold. Heat shimmered visibly in the air around her. The radiance of this goddess made us gasp. And in no time she had waded in, submerged, and then swum out.

Rob was next. Yanking off his shirt he whooped, as he often did, his exuberance unchecked, and struggled out of his jeans even as he ran. His penis freed and bobbing happily, he stormed into the clear green icy water, stirring up a froth. He whooped again. Wildly he kicked and stroked in big noisy bubbly circles, then flipped onto his back, closed his eyes, and barely moved at all. Walter and I stood on the rock and gazed down: Rob's long hair and beard floated out and encircled his ruddy face like a feathery aureole of seaweed. DeeDee swam silently up behind him, dove under, and in seconds he was shrieking and flailing from her pinch.

Walter stripped and went in next, shivering as he forced his skinny white body to submerge. Then I followed. The water was so cold it stung, and so clear I could see every strand of hair on my legs and every pebble on the lake floor. I threw myself all the way in, backstroked strongly until I warmed up, then I floated and watched the deepening blue of sky directly above. Through a break in the ring of trees around the lake shone the last afterglow of what had been a blazing orange sun. I paddled slowly back in lazy sidestrokes. When I returned to shore Walter had already put on his jeans and was intently rolling a joint. I put on my underpants and shirt and sat beside him.

"Wow," he said. "This place is, like, amazing."

The light was fading. DeeDee and Rob were still splashing and cavorting quite far out. Their murmurs and shrieks floated back to us.

"No one else comes here?" I asked.

"We've never seen a soul."

"Now you'd see us. Too bad it's so far," I said.

Walter laughed. He twisted the end of the joint and examined it. His thick glasses were smudged with fingerprints. He said, "Where it is is where it is. Where it is is like part of, you know, the whole picture. If it were closer, it wouldn't be here. You know what I mean? If we could get here every day it wouldn't be this lake."

He lit the joint and inhaled deeply. He nudged me to take it from him, leaning his shoulder onto mine. As if for warmth. Like puppies, I thought, drawing on the joint. We are like puppies.

A deep gurgle of DeeDee's laughter echoed across the water.

Walter gestured toward Rob and DeeDee, reaching out with his goose-bumped arm. His shirt, draped loosely over his shoulders, fell off. "Wow, look at them," he said again, laughing. Then he wriggled into the shirt. I helped.

They had drifted a bit toward shore. Closely facing him, DeeDee clutched her arms around Rob's neck. Somewhere underwater he must have had his arms around her waist. Circling that fertile belly? I took another hit. And their legs? I wondered calmly to myself. In such a pose, where were the legs? Where was anything else at all?

Rob whooped, threw DeeDee over, pushed her down, dove down with her. Not puppies, I thought. Those two are not like puppies.

"Man, to just let it all go and submerge," said Walter, shaking his head. "Sonia, this is part of the vision, isn't it? Really *really* part of the vision."

"What vision?" I said.

A foot broke the surface of the water from underneath and kicked into the air. Was it his or hers? I couldn't tell.

"You know. The *vision*."

My mind was peeling off in soft shreds. A vision. I forgot. Right now it didn't seem to matter much, that I'd forget a vision. Forget to *have* a vision. Someday it might matter. Someday it definitely *would*, I sensed it; placidly I foresaw that far-off future urgency as I inhaled on the joint. But right now Walter had his vision, and that would do.

DeeDee shot up from underwater, thick dark ropes of wet hair completely covering her face. She roared with laughter, catching her breath. She waved to us. "Hi guys!" she called out, still masked completely by soppy curls. Then she disappeared again, as if Rob, from down below, needing no air, had yanked her by her feet.

Her feet? But why did I think it was her feet?

"Not puppies," I said aloud.

"Huh? What puppies?" asked Walter. But immediately he let the question go. "A vision of, you know, freedom. We make everything new again. Right? The world is ours to change. Look, we got us outta the war. We refused the tyranny of the suburbs, the rat race. We don't use hardly any of their *stuff*. Betcha we bring down the president. So? Right? Anything is possible."

Now their heads were above water, both of them. DeeDee's voice lilted softly and I strained to hear what she was saying. No way could I make it out. A burst of Rob's loud laughter followed, then his voice dropped to a low confiding murmur.

"Anything is possible," I repeated.

"We make it up as we go along. It's all new." Again Walter nudged me with his bony shoulder, grinning widely, taking back the smoldering remnant of the joint.

• • •

Seasons came and went, the years, too. Carelessly we let several blow away, as if the supply was inexhaustible.

In any winter ours was no ordinary cat. Though lithe and capable of weightless acrobatics outdoors, when she curled atop the quilts which in turn were piled atop a leg or foot, this cat acquired a formidable mass and weight. A stony lump of unmatched density, she could trap and pin a two-hundred-pound six-foot-two man. The colder the night, the heavier and more unbudgeable the cat. When she conspired with the dog, two concrete slabs immobilized us both. Wedged between or under them, we were helpless, the timbers holding up the house put to the test.

In the middle of a deeply cold night, Rob tried to turn over, but the mass of animal slumber resisted and bore down. Still asleep, he struggled, dislodged, and flipped from right to left. The cat lump rolled along without opening its eyes and asserted its triumphant presence in a new leg spot downhill; but the dog bulk protested. She yelped, she growled, frenetically she scratched with two front paws to arrange the cloth into a nest at my feet, just so. She plopped onto it with a loud groan. But still it wasn't right: she scrambled to her feet, dug furiously, then resettled in a tight curl, emitting a tremulous and melancholy sigh. In seconds, as she fell asleep, she metamorphosed into several hundred tons of unmovable dead weight.

We finally drifted back to sleep, too, weighted down by our darling animals like flowers pressed for posterity under ponderous tomes. The house settled into its just tolerable temperature, the stove banked to simmer quietly until morning. Above all we did not want to rouse from the gentleness of our dreams to handle wood. No matter how ferocious the cold or wind, the final stoking before bedtime was carefully, minutely calculated and arranged so we would not have to cast off the sanctity of our quilts or set foot on the cold floor or be traumatized by the roughness of bark on our skin or gauge the heft of logs to fit inside the stove. In sleep we were not responsible. So through the night, untended, the mellowest embers persisted until dawn, making their slow journey to the finest ash by way not of fast, crass flames but of patient low-sizzling red-striated coals.

But in the middle hours of our night, Wiggle woke cold to the dreaming house. She trotted silently from our feet to our heads and sniffed and schnuffled at each of our faces. A cold wetness on my nose awoke me, but I kept my eyes shut, pretended to sleep. She burrowed that inquisitive snout under the top quilt, then the lower one, and then she wriggled her whole body underneath. She slunk down and nestled against our legs. She rolled herself up one way, then the other, seeming to turn herself inside out. Finally she settled in again. But just as I was drifting off, I heard the cat's unmistakable hunting trill, *brrrrrupp*, then a feline paw swatted at the new lump under the quilt. Wiggle squirmed but held firm. The cat tiptoed to my head and pawed her way beneath the covers. Copycat, I thought. She planted herself like a cast iron pillar on my shoulder, tucking her ears under my chin. So be it, I thought; peace at last. But the warmest lower realms must still have called to her. Once I was asleep she edged down. And down still further, until she landed against the dog.

Tumult! War! The quilts bounced up alive, tucked-in corners thrashed to disarray. Snarls and hisses tore through the muffling cloth. They skirmished for prime space: the bend of Rob's right knee. The cat played dirty, grabbed with open claws.

"Shit!" In one syllable, one move, Rob threw off the covers, sprung to his feet. Clutching his leg, he kicked both stunned creatures off the bed.

"Out of here, you guys! *Get lost!*"

They thumped unceremoniously to the floor. Scrambling to their feet, suddenly drawn together in a truce, they stared at us with disbelief, wounded, exiled, and humiliated. I lit the lantern. Rob rolled up one ankle of his long johns: a long thin scratch, with barely any blood, broke the skin. I groped and found the witch hazel, then dabbed it on. We blew out the light, got back into bed, straightened the quilts.

"Good night," I said. "Sweet dreams." I snuggled up against him.

The dog jumped back first, pretending not to, and sentenced herself to the farthest corner near my feet. The cat followed, invisible and weightless, near Rob's. We ignored them.

When I woke an hour later, they were in the center of the bed: Wiggle sprawled lengthwise against my back, the cat curled massively beside her. Rob clutched the very edge of his side of the mattress, I clung to mine.

"Animals," I whispered.

Rob reached across the fur and groped my hand.

5. *Searchers*

Stanley's father, Hannibal, was an odd man. For one thing, he seemed not to mind the outsiders who'd moved to town; for another, he looked like one, or so his oldest neighbors thought, though few outsiders would have been happy with the comparison. His long gray hair was wildly unkempt, his clothes might have been salvaged from the dump; at first glance he could have been a wild man emerging from the forest for the very first time. And yet he could turn the cleverest of phrases and muster a vocabulary that awed his fellow townsmen; certainly he had read widely in something besides the Sears Roebuck catalog, though it was clear that he had read that, too.

When I asked where he got the name Hannibal, he said, "Do you think I'm named after the original?"

"Maybe you're a direct descendant," I teased, because right from the start we had teased.

"My second wife thought I was descended from one of the elephants he took across the Alps. But it was a cousin of my mother's father I was named after, Hannibal Hamlin. Betcha don't know who *he* was." And of course I didn't.

"Why, he was vice-president to Abraham Lincoln!" The way

Hannibal said it, rubbing the whiskers on his chin and mocking me with his bright green eyes, he seemed to be suggesting that he shared a certain greatness not just with Hamlin, but with the president himself.

Still, the pig snorted around the kitchen door and countless vehicles were rusting in his yard. He had been born in his house and had lived there with two different wives, one long dead ("my old man drank my mother to death," Stanley told me) and one long departed to a house far up the road. And there he had fathered six children: Stanley, Linda, and the four younger ones who still lived with their mother. For twenty-five years he'd been tax assessor of the town, and a few months each year he worked on the state road crews patching up the holes, and between the two jobs he never had to sit inside very long and he made as much money as he ever needed, assuming he had long ago stopped supporting any kids.

One day in spring when Rob and Stanley cut wood together, I went to pick Rob up, but they hadn't yet returned. Hannibal was sitting on the steps of his back doorway, deep in thought, elbows on his knees, chin resting in his hands. The back-step philosopher. When his blind mutt began to bark, Hannibal saw me.

"Blind old bastard sees better than I do," he said, scooting over on the broken step. I sat next to him.

"You got your peas in yet?" he asked, staring out at his own garden, where last year's weeds were still a tangled mess.

"Two weeks ago," I said.

"Huh," he said. "Then you'll get tired of them faster."

I laughed. "Uh-uh. Not me."

"Well," he said. "You get too far ahead of a season around here, you only wind up in winter that much sooner." He winked at me.

"So," I replied, "that means you must keep out of winter altogether."

"Damn right," he said gruffly, but he squinted at me with a flicker of appreciation.

We talked about the Dinkins place. I asked him if he'd known Matt Dinkins, the one murdered by his sister.

"Never knew him except when he was a little tot. But the whole family had a curse on it, it seems. I knew the old grandfather before they locked him up."

"They locked him up?"

Hannibal crushed a cigarette and thrust his fists into the pockets of his flimsy jacket. "He lived back there, at your place, all alone. There were still some houses along that road, but not many, and he kept to himself. People got to thinking he was queer. Kids from the Howell place and a coupla others, they used to come and make sport of him. I don't actually know if he was all that crazy *before* they started treating him like he was."

"That happens," I said.

"That happens," he repeated. He took his hands from his pockets. They were red, wrinkled, and raw. He fumbled for a Lucky Strike from a crumpled packet and offered me one. I declined. He lit his, took a long draw on it and flung the dead match out into the dusk, which was about to swallow us up in filmy grayness.

"So," he began again. "They'd come around at night and call out funny noises, y'know, like it was Halloween or some such thing, only it wasn't. And then they took to knocking on his windows, first one side of the house, then the other. He'd rush out the front, then run around to the back, but by then they were gone. It wasn't nice, but they were just kids." He threw the cigarette off into the bushes. "They weren't nice kids, but they were kids." He looked off to the last glimmer of light in the sky and thought in silence. Then he said, "Christ, my own nephew was one of them. He grew up to be a mean son-of-a-bitch, but he *was* only a kid when he was a kid." He waited for the roar of a passing pulp truck to fade away. I was freezing.

"So it was the windows, I think, that did it to him. The kids tapping on the windows late at night. It got so that even when the wind rattled the glass, he'd rush out angry. He didn't know the wind from the kids anymore. And one night he was waiting with his rifle. Somebody pounded on a window, and it wasn't the wind, and Dinkins shot back."

"Ouch," I said.

"Killed a twelve-year-old boy. A Gilligan boy."

"And that's when they locked him up?"

"Yup. For a time. Then it seems they didn't see a point to keeping a crazy old bastard in prison all his life. So they let him out. He finished up in a trailer down in Pineland." Hannibal shook his head. "A trailer."

We sat in silence for a minute, then Stanley's truck turned in the driveway. Hannibal stood up. So did I. He said to me, "For Chrissakes, watch those windows back there, will ya?" And he disappeared into his house.

• • •

It was a nasty, stormy night and I was alone: Rob had left for a week to see his family. The wind howled and the house shook with each gust. Wiggle paced uneasily back and forth across the floor, her little claws going *click-click-click* on the wood planks. She made me more uneasy than I'd been. I tensed. She sensed my tension and her *click-click-click* became more frantic.

"Quit it, Wiggle!" I commanded. "Sit!" I patted my lap. She jumped on. We huddled by the stove, holding onto one another, but the house was not the least bit cold.

And that was when I heard the pounding on the west window. I jumped. Wiggle leaped off my lap and barked a high-pitched, ululating bark. I opened the door and she flew out, snarling and snapping beneath the window. But from the doorway the darkness was total; I could not make out a single form, not of trees, not of sheds, not of wild animals or intruders in the night. Wiggle came back in and began again to pace. I grabbed her and forced her on my lap. "Sit still!" I yelled. A low growl rumbled in her throat. I opened a book and tried to read, but not a word sank in. The wind whistled in the fir trees behind us.

Knock-knock-knock! Again there was the pounding on the window. Wiggle and I both sprung out of the chair, ran to the door, and flew outside. I went right up to the window. No one was there. I tried to see into the trees, but in the faint rectangle of light cast through the window from the lanterns inside, I discerned only the vaguest gray outline of branches.

Wiggle and I went back in. She lay down beside the stove with a groan, and I changed out of my soaked clothes. A huge gust of wind sent a tremor through the house and all the windows rattled.

"See," I said out loud to Wiggle. "It's just the wind."

Wiggle sighed, flopped over to her other side, and groaned again.

"Ssssh," I said. "It's nothing but the wind."

And then the wind picked up even more, pine boughs lashed harder against the walls, and the outhouse door came loose. It banged open, it banged shut, the hinges squealed. Wiggle's ears flew up in two straight lines.

"Sssh," I said. "It's nothing."

And that was when I heard the laughter, children's giggles, unmistakable.

"Oh God, it's *them!*" I cried. "It's those *kids!*"

Wiggle let out a squeaky yip and jumped into my lap.

• • •

There was something different about Stanley. It took me a minute to notice.

"Well, for Chrissakes, aren't you gonna let me in?" He stood in the doorway stomping his feet, his hands in the pockets of his hunting jacket and his rifle leaning against the woodshed. He had no gloves on; probably he owned no gloves. He had no "real" winter clothes, just the same jacket the whole year round and God knows how many long johns underneath.

He blew on his knuckles, swiveled a chair over by the stove, and sat with his feet right inside the warming oven. He had set the rifle on the wood box.

"Rob's not here?" he asked.

"Uh-uh." It was the first time he had ever visited me alone. "It's some mean cold," I said, and I slid a mug of coffee over to him.

"Naah," he answered with his usual sarcasm. "It's Miami Beach." He looked at me half mockingly, half expectantly, and finally I *saw*.

"Stanley! The glasses!"

"Well Je-sus H. Christ. It took you long enough."

"Wire-rims? *You?*"

He gulped down the coffee. "Now it's *me* gotta look like a goddamned bookworm."

"They're not *reading* glasses, are they?"

He sat up indignantly. "You don't think I can read?"

I laughed. I was the only person Stanley allowed to laugh at him, so I let my laughter stretch out. "Stanley, come off it. Do you see any better?"

"Yeah. Maybe if I'd had 'em in 'Nam I would've aimed better."

I frowned. "Or maybe you would have seen the light."

He sneered. "Don't start on me, for Chrissakes. I nearly got killed over there. Lotsa my buddies came home in bags. And you—you were back here in your stupid peace marches."

I leaned back in my chair. "Not quite. You've got me confused with someone else. I was in Europe when you were in Vietnam."

"Shit!" he said. "Europe!" He yanked his feet out of the warming oven. I smelled the overheated rubber. "And what were you doing *there?*" he asked contemptuously.

I sighed. "Working with deserters, Stanley. Americans. Hiding them until they had a safe place to go."

He slammed his hand on the table. "Christ, I should've known."

I didn't want a fight. Not here, alone with Stanley and his gun. "This peace stuff," I said. "It all started with my first pair of glasses."

He sneered again.

"You'll see," I said. "It'll catch up with you, too."

"Shit," he said, jumping to his feet.

"Anyway, we rub off on people, if they're around us long enough."

"Not *me* you don't!" he shouted, fastening the top button of his jacket.

"I don't know about that, Stanley. You *do* seem to keep coming back."

"Shit, that's only because you make the only decent coffee this side of Pineland."

"Yeah, I suppose." I grinned at him. "Sure."

"Leave me the hell alone!" he hollered, opening the door. The wind blew through the woodshed, right inside to me. He stuck his hands in his pockets, stepped out onto the icy path, and turned back with the sneer still on his face.

"Those glasses," I called out. "They look pretty damn good."

"Ya think so?"

"Yup," I said.

He smiled.

"Now go hit the books," I said.

"Oh for Chrissakes." He stomped off through the snow.

• • •

We called him Shithead, and he hunted birds. He left his pick-up at our driveway and took his dog into the woods, but not far, just at the edge of our gardens and orchards so we couldn't see them but could still hear the steady tinkle of the dog's bell as they kept circling our clearing. The man yelled at the dog a lot. Sometimes he shot at birds. Sometimes we yelled at him to get further from the house. Wiggle went nuts with all the noise. I would yell at my own dog to shut up. This went on day after day.

When it started up again the following year, I went up to Shithead as he got into his pick-up. "Listen," I told him, "keep away from the house."

And Shithead said, "The land's not posted, I can hunt wherever I want."

I said, "That's *why* land gets posted." He smirked. I said, "There's a mile of nothing to the north and a mile of nothing to the south and a mile of nothing to the east and a mile of nothing to the west, so hunt *there* and keep the hell away from my house."

He scowled at me and drove away.

I kept waiting for him to come back and murder me. That year he stayed away. The next year, though, he came back, the dog tinkling and Shithead himself shouting and shooting at the very edge of our gardens.

• • •

Mike and Jean came up from New York City. Mike had been a conscientious objector; they met each other leafletting during the war. After a few summers camping in a teepee on their land, they built a house and settled. Mike had a little building just for writing poetry in. Life was good. When the big tomcat from down the road started hassling their cats, Mike would shoot his gun into the air to scare it.

"You shouldn't do that," I said. "You never know where the bullet lands."

"Oh come on," he said. "It just goes into that back field."

"How do you know nobody's back there?"

"Nobody's ever back there."

"It would be better if you just shot the tom," I said.

• • •

Everett had been a blacksmith and was legendary for his skill, tremendous strength, and violent drunken sprees. Now he was silent and burned out. But he always planted corn a week or two before anyone else, and it always worked. I saw in the exuberance and symmetry of his garden the suggestion of the artist in him that, given room somewhere else, might have grown to an enormous talent. But what happened to a personality cornered in a fixed and narrow place, unable to branch, was that it simply grew more and more layers on the old theme until its texture became its chief quality — instead of something expanded and more varied, it was more and more of its own essence. Even Everett's silence, turned in and intensified upon itself for so many years, achieved a solidity, a mass and weight.

We would see him on the highway and he would wave in a very slow and deliberate way. One fall we picked potatoes acres apart on the same field and we would wave. During a soft Thanksgiving snow we met him at the end of our road; he was on foot, hunting silently. Even then, so close, we waved.

Finally one year during hunting season he parked at our driveway and came down to the house, leaving his gun in his truck. It was 8 A.M. We invited him in. He entered but refused coffee. With few words, he asked if it was okay to hunt back in our woods. It was okay. His eyes darted around the house, taking in the golden pine walls, the bright drapes, the fieldstone chimney, the stove, the immense and sunny windows. I could see the impression of each detail strike him.

He walked over to the chimney and ran his hand along the rocks. He tapped at the mortar seams. He stood back and examined the chimney from a few feet, walked all the way around it, and stroked it again. He said, "That's quite a smokestack." And then, slowly and deliberately, he nodded his head and left.

• • •

Rob was splitting wood when he heard the truck at the top of the hill, the green truck with no muffler, and by the time he got up there it was parked at the only possible angle that could block our driveway. Millard Worlsley was already marching down the road, rifle in hand, eager to make good on the last day of hunting season.

Rob yelled, "Hey, Worlsley. Get your truck out of my driveway."

"You goin' someplace?" Millard yelled back.

"Get it outta there, Worlsley."

"Shit, you can get around me!"

"It's a stupid place to put it, Millard."

If Millard Worlsley hated anything it was to be called stupid. Even from the lower garden, where I was tearing up cornstalks and pumpkin vines, I could hear Millard snarl. And then his truck started up with a roar, it moved, it stopped, and Rob went back to splitting wood.

It was one of those cold, sunny autumn days when voices carried clear as birdsong, when you wanted to get everything done for winter and felt you almost could. But clouds were amassing over the hills in the northwest. If it stayed cold, we'd have the season's first snow by morning. If it warmed up, there would be rain and mess, the frost already in the ground would soften, the road would turn to quicksand, the gardens would be mush. I hoped for snow.

Just before sundown Rob came down with the wheelbarrow to haul away the last of my vines. "Shit, Worlsley's truck is still there. If he gets stuck out in the woods all night, he'll be sorry."

Millard knew the woods, how to get in and out of them and how to get what he wanted out of them. Like most of the homesteaders he was a rebel of the sixties, except that what *he* rebelled against was a father who was professor of philosophy in some Midwestern university and two older brothers who were conscientious objectors during the war. So Millard became a gun freak and a slob. He loved making people squirm. He'd sidle into any conversation with talk of ammunition and his guns. His aesthetic was the beauty of a shot aimed to the heart. The shame of his life was that he'd been kept out of Vietnam for reasons he refused to discuss. But he wasn't stupid. He'd go red in his pudgy face if his lack of education began to show, and he made it clear that if he looked ignorant, it was someone else's fault for setting things up to make him seem so.

Natalie was Millard's first wife; he was her third husband. Her first was killed in a car wreck; the second blew his brains out. She didn't have much luck with husbands. She was fat and nearly as broad as the truck they puttered around in, and she had a soft, doting heart, so she took in strays: cats, dogs, men. We'd heard she'd had miscarriages, one after another, and children were obviously what she *should* have had. Instead she let her cats breed, she let dust bloom and junk pile up and sorrows multiply. She got a cashier's job at a local diner and paid the bills, while Millard always professed to have a big deal in the works.

They were not your average backwoods hippie couple.

Night fell. We listened to news on the radio and had our dinner. When we looked out into the dark, there was the faint metallic glimmer of Millard's truck up on the hill.

We went up to the truck. The air was warm and heavy, it seemed to cling right to our skin. "Mil-lard!" We yelled his name into the night, but no answer followed. "Worls-ley!" Our voices were swallowed into the mist. Just as we reached the door of the house, the rain began its soft descent.

We could not debate too long. Maybe Millard deserved a night out in the rain, for being stupid and greedy enough to follow tracks long after he should have known to turn back. But for every scenario of Millard's greed, we could picture a thousand accidents, the misfired shot. He seemed, anyway, to carry his own death around with him, like a pebble in his shoe, and he must have had just the smallest irritation, the reminder of it, always there.

"Some fuckin' woodsman," Rob grumbled as we got into the car. Already the ground was softening, the tires slid along the road as if we were riding on butter. And the darkness was flat, without shadows or depth; it drew itself around us, an impenetrable gray shroud.

Outside Natalie's trailer, the Great Dane snapped and snarled at us, straining at the end of a rope. Two sheepdogs barked gruffly, the little black curly mongrel came yapping at our ankles as soon as Natalie opened up the door.

"Careful of the lumber," she warned. We stepped around the jumbled pile of two-by-fours and plywood that were the next stage of a house Millard had been building a long time.

"Damn yard light's out," she said, and she laughed nervously. She stood in the doorway, making it hard for us to pass inside. She wore a huge tent of a housedress.

Inside, her ashtray was piled high with butts. The room was dim and clogged with overstuffed chairs. In the murkiness, the sheepdogs threw themselves down alongside the stove, grunted, and stared at us warily. A heap of small black kittens mewed in a basket behind the stove, and huge round furry cats kept walking through the room. The trailer smelled strongly of wet fur and smoke.

"Oh, he's okay," said Natalie bravely when we told her about Millard. "He never got a damned thing this year, so he couldn't resist one last try. Went too far in to get out before dark." She stomped out one cigarette, then lit another. "Damn fool," she said again. She laughed in her deep, throaty way, keeping her eyes on the big white cat in her lap. "He'll be okay." She stroked the cat. Then she looked up at me. "Won't he?"

"We'd like to call the game wardens," Rob said. "They could find him and guide him out."

"There's no need," said Natalie. The white cat jumped off her lap. An orange one jumped on. "Is there?"

"To be on the safe side," I said.

"The damn fool," she said.

"Can I use your phone?" asked Rob.

The tears came to Natalie's eyes. It was as if Millard would only be in trouble if we went ahead and called. "Sure," she said.

The wardens said they'd be up our road in a few minutes. Natalie wanted to stay home and wait. "He could come barging in the door the minute you leave!" She laughed her husky laugh.

So we went back. We left the car at the end of our road and walked the mile in. The rain was heavy now and cold, but not cold enough to turn to snow. Our feet began to get sucked down in the mud.

"Damn!" yelled Rob. "The wardens'll rip the shit out of the road!"

Less than half an hour later they came churning up through the mud in a four-wheel-drive jeep. We met them at the top of the driveway and showed them Millard's truck, then they went churning off farther up the road towards the Howell place. We heard them fire shots to signal to Millard where they were. We heard no signal back. The wardens were in the dark rainy woods for over an hour.

They knocked on the door, standing in their big yellow slickers with rainwater cascading down their faces. "No sign of 'im," said one. They came in to warm up by the stove. "He could've walked out another way. He could still be in there fine 'n dandy. But there ain't no way to search on a night like this but by signals." He sighed, then blew on his knuckles. "If he ain't back in the morning, we'll try again." They agreed to go tell Natalie. They left puddles on the floor all around the stove. We heard the jeep straining through the mud as they left. It was midnight.

At four-thirty I woke to the sound, first, of Rob hissing, "Worlsley!" then the roar of the mufflerless truck. It roared once, it roared again, we could hear the tires spinning in the mud.

We went up the hill. Millard slid out of the rut he was in and began churning up a new one.

"Jesus Christ, Millard, where the hell were you? Quit making ruts!" Rob yelled.

Millard turned off the engine and leaned out of the truck, grinning smugly. His clothes looked dry enough. "Spent the night in the woods," he said. "I made a lean-to outta branches and lit a fire. It wasn't bad."

"You bastard," I said. "You had everyone worried to death. Natalie must be a wreck by now."

Millard kept grinning.

Rob said, "Didn't you hear the wardens firing signals?"

"Guess not," said Millard. He started up the truck again.

Over the roar Rob yelled, "Don't drive down the road now, Worlsley. You'll put ruts in worse than anyone can fix. Christ, the wardens coming in after you did enough of a job."

"Natalie's real worried," said Millard. He waved, revved up the engine once more, and spluttered out of the rut and away, sending mud flying and chewing up the road into deep troughs.

Two weeks later they came up the road on foot; Natalie must have been pushing him every step of the way. "He wants to apologize," said Natalie, falling heavily into a chair. She was panting, but before she caught her breath she lit a cigarette. Her face was gray. Millard paced around the kitchen. He picked up a bread knife and fondled it.

"Damn it," Natalie said. "Millard, *say* something!"

He was looking down at the floor. "I'm sorry I put ruts in the road," he mumbled. And when he looked back up at us, he smirked.

"He wants to help smooth out the ruts," said Natalie.

"It's frozen now," said Rob.

"In the spring, then," said Natalie.

"Sure," said Rob. He sighed. "In the spring."

It was not that spring but the one after: Millard finished enough of the house so they could move in. There was still tar paper on the outside, and the inside walls were silvery with insulation, but they brought in everything that had been squeezed into the trailer, including the four dogs and eleven cats.

A few weeks later while Natalie was at work and Millard was out somewhere looking for it, the house caught fire. A fierce wind wound the flames around it like a ribbon, and the volunteers arrived too late. When they opened what was left of the front door, the little black curly mongrel came flying out, screaming but unhurt. All the other pets burned up inside.

6. Patriots

WE WERE PACKED INTO THE chicken coop again for Watergate, a dozen of us glued to the screen again, heckling again. Jeff went all solemn in his mimicry of Alexander Butterfield. "'I was aware of listening devices, yes sir.'"

We all laughed as we already had several times at this performance.

"Taping every conversation! God, why didn't they just take home movies of it all!"

"They probably did, just nobody's discovered them yet."

Events were barreling along at a fast clip. We were still reeling from the news of the enemies lists, the spying on antiwar groups (as if we hadn't known), the tapes. During commercial breaks, Genie and Jeff, who'd mastered all the punch lines, re-enacted the precious tidbits for those of us who'd spent less time here.

Lamely impersonating John Dean, Genie made her face go blank and earnest, grabbing for my glasses and setting them on her nose. "Yes sir, we made an effort to use the available federal machinery to screw our political enemies."

"Yes indeed, all the available federal machinery!" echoed Jeff.

"We strafed Ellsberg's office."

"We defoliated his backyard. That maximized our use of the available federal machinery."

"We were about to drop the most advanced weapons system on SDS headquarters, but you spoiled it with this silly investigation, sir."

"Wait, hold on—" Rob pointed back to the TV screen—"Here's Weicker, giving hell to Strachan."

Now we were trying to absorb the news that among the enemies, there were friends: one hundred *Democratic* members of Congress who did not, in their 1972 bid for re-election, "receive very strong opposition from Republicans."

As we were sinking our teeth into this latest revelation, Hannibal dropped in. Jeff's roach clip quickly disappeared from sight. While grizzled Hannibal, reeking of bad whiskey, was not exactly a paragon of civic rectitude, he was still a tax assessor and therefore allied in our minds and nightmares with Authority. Jeff put an innocent bag of popcorn into circulation. Without disturbing the baby at her breast, Genie maneuvered the two-year-old onto her lap, too, and scooted over so Hannibal could sit on the couch and not test his arthritis down on the floor with all the rest of us. Unabashedly, he strained for a glimpse of Genie's nipple.

"...Republicans doing in Republicans!" exclaimed Weicker.

Rob slapped his knee. "Un-fucking-believable!"

Weicher was about to pop a blood vessel. "Did we have *any* sort of election contest? Was there a contest in 1972 for the House or Senate?"

"Poor Connecticut flatlander," said Hannibal. "All this time he thought there was a difference between Republicans and Democrats."

Rob objected, "Well, there's a *little*."

Hannibal guffawed. "The Democrats put the unions right in Nixon's pocket, God bless 'em, and who for Chrissakes has kept that war afloat, troops or no troops?"

"Yeah, but *this*"—Rob gestured to the TV screen, the entire Watergate performance—"we wouldn't have had *this* without Republicans."

"Or secret bombing in Cambodia," added Jeff.

Hannibal laughed again. "They're all crooks, they've always all been crooks, they always all will be crooks. You think it isn't *always* like this? You think a circus investigation into these *particular* dirty tricks will *change* anything?"

Ever the believer in the rightability of wrongs, Rob spluttered in protest. And I wondered: was it possible that Hannibal, the sixty-year-old Downeast tax assessor from whom we hid our marijuana, our atheism, and our true non-marital status, was more of a revolutionary than my own dear love?

"Those are anarchist words," chided Jeff.

"Suit yourself," Hannibal retorted.

On the screen, Strachan was still squirming. But so were we.

"A sideshow," said Hannibal. "They'll pretend to clean it up. Then watch. It will be business as usual. Dirty tricks up the kazoo and nobody'll be looking for another twenty, thirty years."

We munched silently on our popcorn. Genie took the baby off her breast, pulled her shirt down discreetly to cover herself, and fought off the other kid's groping hands.

"Lemonade anybody?" Jeff asked.

There were no takers for lemonade. No more hecklers either. No breasts, no joints. We kept our eyes glued on Strachan and Weicker.

"Anyway," said Hannibal after a long while, as he scooped up a handful of popcorn, "you can smell that weed halfway to Bangor, you'd need forty tons of Air Wick to chase it outta here." He chewed on popcorn, then swallowed. "Or else bring them chickens back into this coop. That'd do it."

• • •

"Make way!" ordered DeeDee, stepping over Katie's legs, squeezing in between Rob and David, the baby fast asleep in the carrier on her chest. She grinned around at everybody, blew a kiss to me, then nestled close to Rob.

It was the second summer, and we gathered at the same TV. On the same floor. In the same chicken coop. With the same piles of lumber and fixtures waiting patiently outside. Genie and Jeff's three-year-old was nearly weaned now and only took the breast once or twice a day. Their little one, given to sudden manic spurts of shrieking and dervish-like spinning, still glomped onto Genie for hours at a stretch. And Genie was pregnant again. It was August; despite the heat, we squeezed in close. There was no choice. Mosquitos buzzed inside and out; a loud smack on flesh would crackle now and then. Hannibal took his honored place beside Genie on the couch. Again, he aimed his sideways glances clearly to the stunning brown aureole of her breast. Popcorn, granola cookies, home-brewed beer, and wine all made the rounds. Walter set in motion a plate of brownies too, into which, we understood without a spoken word, he'd baked some hash. Then he sat down next to me.

Stanley ducked in at the last minute and stayed right at the door, on his feet, leaning against the wall at a strained acute angle that kept his head from hitting the ceiling but must have given him a sharp cramp in his side.

"Hey Stanley, there's at least two or three inches of space here for you," called Patty, patting the floorboard. "Come sit with us."

Stanley scowled, then took a long gulp of beer without budging from his wall.

"Sssh," said Rob. "The *man* is starting."

We quieted for a moment and focused on the screen. Nixon was tense as he began. "This is the thirty-seventh time I have spoken to you from this office…"

"Wow, look at *that* big gleaming forehead," said Genie. "You think his hair has receded more since the thirty-sixth time he spoke to us?"

"I can't believe I'm watching this," I said. "After all these years, avoiding the sight of that face."

"Like going to the funeral," said Walter, swallowing a piece of brownie. "Of somebody you couldn't stomach alive."

"Shut up, you guys," snarled Stanley.

"…there is no longer a need for the process to be prolonged," Nixon intoned solemnly.

"Who's prolonging it, you asshole?" shouted Jeff. "Just get outta here!"

Stanley shouted back. "Can't you guys shut up and let the man talk?"

"Nobody's stopping him," said Genie softly.

"Stanley, you can't dictate—" began Sheldon, but then he too was cut off by somebody else's "Ssssh!"

"...would have preferred to carry through to the finish, whatever the personal agony it would have involved..."

"Is he kidding? Who's in agony here? Are we supposed to worry that *he's* suffering?"

Sheldon said, "Maybe the napalm victims in Vietnam will feel sorry for *him*."

"What do you know about that?" hollered Stanley. "Goddamn chickenshit bastard couldn't even let us stay and finish the job." Nobody answered.

"I have never been a quitter..."

"Oh please, don't say that now—"

"Ssssh, let's hear it!"

"...abhorrent to every instinct in my body."

"He has a body?" Katie asked.

"He has an instinct?" I asked.

"Therefore, I shall resign the Presidency effective at noon tomorrow."

And before he could even say the words, "Vice President Ford," we'd burst out in whoops and cheers and loud applause. The babies shrieked. Walter stomped his vibram-soled boots noisily on the floor. Genie clinked a spoon against a gallon jar of fermenting herbs.

Outside, dogs howled and barked in solidarity. Standing high above us, Jeff popped the cork off a bottle of cheap champagne, letting the foam overflow into paper cups and spray onto our heads.

"Shit," sneered Stanley. "What a bunch of morons!" He stomped out, slamming the door.

I felt a tug of something not quite guilt, not quite annoyance, not quite sympathy, as I registered his disgust and solitariness, the latter too defiant to come from mere loneliness, yet too total to be sustained by simple pride. But I couldn't let myself get swallowed up in it. Hannibal didn't fret over his son either; he was as giddy as all the others now, leaning over to give Genie a big kiss. I gratefully surrendered to euphoria too. In that moment, chug-a-lugging champagne, we felt victorious, a triumph not of any personal achievements but of the change that was in the air for everyone, as if, once again, anything was possible and wrongs could be righted and anyone, even any one of us, could change the world. That sense of infinite possibility—we glimpsed it again, we could taste it again, we could almost reach out and touch it, grasp it, feel it palpably it in our hands, almost! A glimpse of infinity in a split second, it danced a teasing dance in front of us, before things would once again close in.

• • •

Again time passed. It was the end of April the next year, 1975. Again we congregated in the chicken coop to watch TV. Genie cradled a new baby at her breast. The four-year-old was entirely weaned now; the two-year-old still nursed. Herbal potions bubbled in their jars in the usual place along one shelf. The windows were open, the screens not yet in; mercifully it was too early for bugs. Strands of fiberglass drooped down from the ceiling where Jeff's head had broken through the insulation's foil wrap. Outside, the piles of two-by-fours and once-new boards had weathered to a gray not unlike the oldest salvaged lumber stacked in other piles. The pews still stood vigil at the herb garden, though one was now atilt against the other. Intricate configurations of copper pipes, a toilet bowl, and a huge enamel sink had joined them. And freshly flattened dirt and a wide circle of stumps, like some ancient burial ground, marked where Jeff had dug postholes and sunk posts and filled the holes back in. The foundation was ready. The fixtures were ready. The lumber was ready. Everything was ready for the real home, the dome.

On the six o'clock news we watched Saigon fall, the North Vietnamese swoop in, the hordes of desperate Southerners trying to flee. Crowds surged at every entrance of the American Embassy. Crowds surged at every available means of transport, swarming onto trucks and boats. Helicopters, packed to capacity, rose into the sky, leaving thousands of shocked and frantic people stranded on the ground. North Vietnamese soldiers moved quickly and effortlessly into town, victorious but confused.

Stanley leaned against the door, wincing at the smiling faces of North Vietnamese troops. "Just like that," he said. He slapped his thigh. "Just like that, the place is overrun. What in God's name was any of it for?"

Aircraft carriers were abuzz, helicopters stirred up dust, movement and crowds and dust and confusion filled the screen. The panic of a people became a roaring, inchoate, televised blur. Yet inevitable. Years and years and hundreds of thousands of deaths too late. And inevitable.

Saigon fell in just one day. How could that be? How could all these years of war, all those dead and maimed, all those protests, all those righteous proclamations, all those schisms between parent and child and north and south and young and old and right and left and east and west come down to just one day? Impossible. And yet people fled Saigon in complete chaos, taken by surprise. They did not expect it. Neither, somehow, did we. Silently, without heckling, without popcorn or dope or drink, but for most of us with some relief, we watched. It was over. After all these years, it was over. The North had won.

"They knew it was coming. How could they not know?" asked Rob.

"You should have seen them bolting from Danang the other day," said Jeff.

"Damn," said Hannibal.

"In days it's over," said Genie.

"That was no days," said Stanley.

"Years and years and years," I said. "Bodies and bodies and bodies."

"But finished in a day."

"In a second. The end of anything is a second."

"Liberation. It had to happen!" Jeff proclaimed.

"Shit!" sneered Stanley.

"The moment of truth," said Patty.

Lowering himself into a crouch beside the door, Stanley hissed, "Truth. You want truth? I'll give you some truth."

"Don't, Stanley," I blurted, sensing a dangerous taunt. "It's enough."

He shot me an angry look. "Be quiet." He drew in a breath, his face an eerie palor. "This is the truth. Listen to it, damnit. I had to fire on civilians. It wasn't a mistake either. It wasn't night, it wasn't the jungle, it wasn't any goddamn fog. It was clear as day. It *was* day. We knew they were civilians. The village was gone, blown to smithereens by choppers the night before. A stinkin' bloody mess. A few terrified, starving people were hiding. But nothing was left. They couldn't hide. They crouched, like I'm crouching here. My captain said finish the job. Under orders, that's what we did. We chased them down and shot them dead. People, chickens, dogs, whatever moved. My buddies did it and I didn't stop them. I did it too. I was told to do that and I did it. We got medals for it, for Chrissakes." A strange calm smirk contorted his face when he stopped talking. He stood up again, leaned again beside the door.

We were all stunned into silence for a full minute.

Then Katie cried out in anguish, hid her face in her hands.

Sheldon said, "You disgust me."

"You pig," said DeeDee.

"Worse than animals," said Sheldon.

"Those are war crimes," Patty blurted.

Stanley stood there smirking.

"Leave him alone," said Rob. "Can't you see what's happening?"

"The whole war was a war crime. It's not your fault," said Jeff.

"How do you know what's not his fault?" said Patty.

"It's too complicated," said Rob. "Leave him alone."

"Complicated? Hah! It's murder! He dares to gloat over this—" Patty stopped.

Stanley stood there, absorbing the words or letting them ricochet off him, I couldn't tell. He did not stop them. He did not rise to them.

Hannibal said, "You did your duty, son. If you had to do it, you had to do it. You did what you had to do."

And that's when Stanley's smirk vanished and his face suddenly went from deathly pale to raging red. "Duty!" he spat out the word. "That's your fuckin' answer? Christ, duty! That's no answer! You're my father! I'm telling you, we shot women, children, people like my mother, my own kid sisters, *you*, goddamn it, *her*—" he pointed to me, and I jumped—"anybody sitting in this goddamn stinking room. And all you tell me is I did what I had to do. That is not a goddamn answer!"

Hannibal looked dumbfounded, mystified at the attack on *him*. He was silent. Stanley waited. Silence persisted.

Stanley glared at Hannibal. "I want *more* from you."

Hannibal's eyes avoided Stanley's. Silence continued. Finally, barely audible, he muttered, "I don't have any more."

Stanley pounded the wall once with the flat of his hand. The whole chicken coop shook. "I need *more*, damnit, from somebody!"

His shouting stopped. Stanley stopped. He froze there, mortified and unforgiving and unforgiven: immobilized like a statue, a monument to what must have been his own normally silent and bottomless torment. All bravado gone. And somehow Rob and I got to our feet, from different sides of this cluster of people on the chicken coop floor, in unison but as yet unaware that we were doing it at all or doing it together, we stood up and we went to him. At this moment we saw him, Stanley, and we saw each other, us, and for this moment we enacted why we were, after all, in some fundamental way that in the dailiness of physical life we had almost completely forgotten, a couple. A human unit. The one Stanley kept trudging back into the woods to visit and to taunt. Now we went to Stanley, we each hugged him, expecting to be rebuffed. But he let us. He clung to Rob to his left, he clung to me to his right. We led him outside. We sat together in the gloom of dusk, huddled on the one upright pew beside the herbs, all three of us holding one another with no words, no answers, no forgiveness, Stanley letting us hold him while he stared dry-eyed at the night.

• • •

On the Fourth of July of 1976, the Bicentennial, Rob and I did not watch TV. Instead we went to the Grange Hall, which bustled with the town's celebration, festooned with crepe paper streamers of red, white, and blue. The kids gobbled down their beans and brown bread and were already waiting for the fun to start before the grown-ups had barely found places at the long tables. The littlest ones grabbed the streamers and twirled themselves up in them, filling the big room with their giggles and shrieks. Two seats down from me sat Hannibal, who had donned a clean blue work shirt in honor of the holiday and brushed his mane of hair so it was swept off his face and back behind his ears. Next to me and between us, in yet one more truce with his old man, Stanley wolfed down food as if he hadn't eaten in days.

"Je-sus H. Christ," he muttered. "This must be one of them *hippie* salads." He poked shredded cabbage and carrots around his plate with his fork, scorn mixed with distaste contorting his face.

"*I* made that salad," said Patty, who sat across from us.

"It's got stupid nuts in it," said Stanley. "Hippie nuts."

Patty's face turned bright red. "It's *healthy*," she said. "You, especially, Stanley, could use a few more vitamins."

"Vitamins!" boomed Hannibal. He winked at me. "Why if any of us Whites had vitamins, we'd keel right over."

"I wouldn't brag about it," said Patty.

"I wouldn't brag about this salad, either," Stanley mumbled.

"Maybe if you were better fed and healthier," said Sheldon, holding his unlit pipe below his scraggly little beard, "you'd work faster on that truck of mine."

"That truck of yours," said Stanley, "is a piece of shit and always will be."

"You said you'd fix it," said Patty.

"Christ," said Hannibal, "I never saw people so set on buying what's broke." He turned to Phyllis Bailey, next to him on the other side, and said in his commanding voice so we could all hear, "Now I seem to recollect that you offered them a truck that worked just fine."

"Ay-yup," chortled Phyllis. "But problem was we wanted a little money for it."

"Not so little," said Patty, now so perturbed she pushed her own salad around with a fork.

"You get what you pay for," said Stanley.

"If you don't want to do it, Stanley, we'll take it somewhere else," Sheldon replied.

"I'll fix that truck, don't you worry," said Stanley. Then he pushed back his chair, lifted his plate from the table, and stood up. "Gonna go get me some *real* food," he announced, and tromped over to the buffet table. No sooner was he gone than his youngest half-sister, a scrawny blond girl about ten, ran over from the table where she'd been sitting with her mother and sat in his seat, leaning expectantly against Hannibal.

"Now I got a heap of a John Deere tractor been out front for nearly twenty years, and it didn't much work for ten or twelve before that. I could let you have it pretty cheap." Hannibal made it clear he addressed these words to Sheldon but his look went clear around the table.

"I don't need a tractor," Sheldon retorted smugly.

"Oh no?" said Hannibal, feigning surprise. "I haven't seen the one you got there moving lately."

Stanley returned and set his plateful of beans down with a clatter. "Guess I'll fix that tractor after I get done with the truck," he said. "Beat it!" he said harshly to the little girl. She grabbed onto Hannibal, who hoisted her onto his lap.

"I can fix the tractor myself," said Sheldon.

Patty burst out laughing.

Hannibal and I exchanged glances. It wasn't like Patty to break rank so publicly, but we all let it pass. Stanley shoved beans into his mouth. Rob seemed uneasy, like he wanted to change the conversation. I could tell by the way he shifted in his chair. He said, "Looks like the kids are getting ready to give us a show."

At one end of the room they were pushing tables together, clearing the way for what would pass for a small stage.

"You singing with 'em?" Stanley asked the little girl, who rested her head snugly against Hannibal's face, oblivious to his massive beard. She glanced up at Stanley and nodded her head silently. "Then get over there!" he yelled.

She frowned and craned her face to see what Hannibal would say, but Hannibal was staring off into the air. She wriggled down from his lap and flew back to her mother's table, where she lit momentarily, got her mother's kiss, and then made a beeline for the group of kids gathering at the stage. I watched the mother, the woman once Hannibal's wife, her face filled with color and animation. She brightened up her whole table. She was one of those deeply freckled people who never tired, who neighbors could always depend on, who children would always adore and always obey. And you could tell she often got angry and stayed angry, the way the color rose so swiftly in her cheeks. I glanced over to Hannibal, who seemed especially gray. He met my look. And as if he read my mind, and as if Stanley were not sitting right between us, swallowing down his beans, Hannibal said, "Yup. Marriage is a great institution. If you're ready for an institution." He smirked. I smiled. And then the kids began to sing.

We sat through Yankee Doodle, and America the Beautiful, and then Yankee Doodle again. All the grown-ups seemed enraptured, even the table with the big, hardy men—the well-driller, the chicken-farmer, the junkman, and the lumberman. All those burly fellows with their caps still on their heads and the suntans flushing the backs of their necks watched and listened with their full attention. When the kids stopped, Freddie Dinkins gave the thank-yous, led some more applause, and announced that Hannibal White would deliver the Declaration of Independence. Even the tableful of hardy men listened carefully, clapped appreciatively, and sat hushed and ready as Hannibal made his way to the front of the room. The children settled quietly into their chairs. Hannibal withdrew a crumpled bit of paper from his shirt pocket and smoothed it out. He cleared his throat. And the room remained absolutely quiet, awaiting the commanding tones we all knew so well.

But for one very long minute, Hannibal stood in silence, wringing his hands and shifting his weight back and forth from one foot to the other. He pushed his glasses, which I'd never seen before, further up on his nose. He made the gesture of smoothing his hair back from his forehead. His face turned pinker, then pinker still. He cleared his throat again with two gruff *ahems*. The room stayed hushed. And finally, when he held up his bit of paper some distance from his face, what came from his mouth—the mouth of a man who could always find the right word—was the smallest, quietest utterance.

"We hold these truths," he said. And then he stopped. There was a restless stir across the room, I could feel it pass from table to table, but no one spoke. Hannibal cleared his throat once again. "We hold these truths to be self-evident," he said, and the words grew fainter and fainter and finished with a raspy catch somewhere down in his chest. By now his face was flushed a brilliant scarlet.

But how patient the town was! The children sat miraculously still in their chairs. The men in their caps fixed their stares discreetly to the floor. The women did not allow themselves to fuss about removing plates, which would have been the natural thing. Even Hannibal's ex-wife sat politely, with a big, energetic smile across her face that seemed to project her fortitude outward, onto him.

Hannibal took a grimy handkerchief from his back pocket and wiped his forehead. He cleared his throat, stood up straight, and loosened the top button of his shirt. "We hold these truths to be self-evident," he said. His voice was still weak and hoarse, but this time he kept his piece of paper at eye level. He looked at it shaking in his trembling hand, then he looked at the silent crowd, and then he blew out a quick puff of air. "That all men are created equal." With his other hand he grabbed the handkerchief again and swabbed his forehead. "That they are endowed by their Creator with certain unalienable rights," he whispered, "that among these are life, liberty, and the pursuit of happiness."

He paused. A couple of men clapped and whooped, to egg him on. And he managed to rattle through the Preamble without losing his voice, which stayed low, on a squeaky, unwavering note. The men stomped and cheered again. The women hushed them. And then brave Hannibal, fortified by his town's rapt attention, read through the rest of the Declaration, racing across every line with no rhythm, emphasis or pause, barely recognizing the ends of sentences, never changing pitch. He raced and raced and raced until he came to the very end. He stopped. He gave an audible sigh of relief. Then, as he pronounced the name John Hancock—slowly, calmly, majestically—he folded up his damp piece of paper, squeezed it into his left breast pocket, and walked quickly back to his seat.

He stared down at his lap as the town burst into applause so tumultuous, it was as if Thomas Jefferson or John Hancock himself had read those words, or as if Hannibal White had invented the whole speech then and there. The hardy men thumped their fists against the table and whistled, the youngsters hooted and cheered, the women held their clapping hands up high. And Hannibal looked up for a brief instant, took the glasses from his nose, and grinned.

7. Open Season

There was one night. There was the long gentle mile of snow and the *swish-swish-swish* of skis against a total silence. There was the moonlight, there were the shadows of trees, the glimmer of ice on branches, the body moving perfectly on skis, and the breath that came right. Stars, earth, breath, snow. In twenty minutes there was just what it took to make these five years at least, and probably the whole of life as well, exactly why we lived them.

• • •

Just before winter the owls started hooting at each other again, long, hollow, throaty noises in the middle of the night. I could not go back to sleep. The owls swooped down and killed rabbits, and the rabbits let out the most awful, piercing death cries. We kept telling Wiggle not to bark—not to bark at owls hooting, not to bark at rabbits dying, not to bark at hunters. She voluntarily gave up barking at deer: she knew one Wiggle was no use against a forest of deer. She wagged her tail at woodchucks. She ignored moose. But she barked one night at noises in the chicken coop. Rob went out in his bare feet and found a chicken already dead. "Get the gun," he yelled to me.

"It's a raccoon. I've got it cornered."

I was so sleepy. "Keep the dog away from it," I called out hoarsely. "Keep Wiggle away from the quills."

"A raccoon, not a porcupine," he said. "Get the gun, please."

I got the gun and brought it to him. He took it. "Now get the bullets," he said patiently.

I ran back to the house, found bullets, and brought them to him as he stood shivering in the doorway of the chicken coop. They were the wrong bullets. The raccoon got away. It didn't matter. We were never much sure anymore what did.

• • •

It was still another one of our summers, it was still that summer of the Bicentennial. I was out there mulching the squash beds, spreading old straw around the plants racing out from each hill, lifting up the vines and enormous leaves to push more straw underneath. The first yellow blossoms were unfurling. Acorn, butternut, buttercup, orange hubbard, blue hubbard, orange Hakaido, Turks turban: I knew each hill by heart. Then I worked on tomatoes, apologizing as I pinched off side shoots, tying up the main branches to wooden stakes with streamers of ripped-up cotton shirts I got for twenty-five cents a bag at rummage sales in churches I'd never otherwise go into. Small clusters of small fruit peeked out here and there. A few tomatoes looked as if they might be preparing to turn pink, but most were a hard, unyielding deep green. Then I hunkered down for the serious work, picking for that night's farmers' market: purple pole beans, green and yellow bush beans, zucchini, yellow squash, early acorn; white onions and red onions, four varieties of carrots, beets, and new potatoes; green and red chard; herbs to arrange in little bunches. I lined up baskets and buckets to fill.

I was lost tying onion braids and bouquets of thick, rippling chard leaves when I heard a vehicle coming slowly nearer. Not Rob, not the Power Wagon coming from up the road where he'd been cutting wood, but something smaller, tinnier, more precise in sound, coming from down off the highway. I waited. It was Stanley, in the car he usually left at the end.

He slammed the door and raced to the garden, fiercely angry, angry at *me*.

"You don't even *know*, do you?" he shouted. "You live so goddamned far back and out of touch, the rest of the world could blow up and you wouldn't even *know*." His face was purple with rage. Whatever it was I didn't know about—surely it was terrible, surely I must have done it.

"Stanley, whoa, slow down," I said. "No, we've got radio, so we'd probably hear about the end of the world. Public radio'd have it. Something local, maybe not. What's going on?"

He pumped out his cheeks, then let them go slack. "Three days. Three days ago, and you don't even *know*. I gotta come back here myself and tell you fuckers!"

I thought: yes, it has been three, no, four days since we last went out. Stanley's face was overtaken by angry tics.

I walked closer to him. "Okay, then, you better tell me."

He couldn't control his face, the distorted pulls of his mouth and his eyes' raging blinks. He was like a flashing neon sign gone haywire. Finally he shouted, "Hannibal's dead, goddamn it! Fuckin' Sheldon Lardner *accidentally* shot him!"

"*What? No!*" I burst into tears.

Stanley dropped to a crouch at my feet and started to bawl.

• • •

I piece together how it went.

It's dusk, a billowy blue-gray froth of a dusk. Hannibal's out on the doorstep, he's given up swatting at the blackflies, he keeps them away with cigarette smoke and whiskey fumes. The old blind mutt lies at his feet, occasionally jumping out of sleep to chomp frenetically at burrs in her matted hind fur. Hannibal could use some good talk, or even some lousy talk, or even the sound of another human being grunting or breathing or wheezing and gulping whiskey next to him, and though he'd never admit it, he's hoping maybe somebody will drive by and see him and stop. But he's not visible; he's not exactly *in*visible, but the darkness is oozing in, a syrup coating everything, and he has no lights on outside the house. There *are* no lights outside the house; Stanley shot the last one out four years ago.

And while he's staring off into space, gazing at the shredded curlicues of his cigarette smoke, a flash of movement catches his sideways attention. He turns to focus more deliberately on the road again and sees a large dark form moving, moving fast, and realizes one of Linda's horses has gotten free and is heading across the road to Sheldon Lardner's side.

"Shit!" he says and pulls himself to his feet none too energetically, pitching a cigarette butt into the bushes.

The dog gets up too. Hannibal yells, "Stay!" but she trots along at his heels until he hits her nose lightly with one finger. He'll have enough trouble getting that horse back over here, he doesn't need the mutt yipping at their feet. She yelps as if she'd been slapped hard, then sits and cowers, whimpering beside the ditch.

"That's right, feel sorry for yourself, you spoiled whiny thing."

The dog twists around to bite at her hindquarters.

Hannibal ambles across the road. There isn't a vehicle in sight except the Lardners' various wrecks decaying quietly like old tree stumps in their driveway and beside the barn. In the murkiness of the humid night, Hannibal stops and discerns: old house, old barn, half a new stone house, horse. The old house, the one where the Lardners still hole up, is completely dark, curtains drawn. Yet all the vehicles are there.

"I'll be Jesus," he mutters. "They're already in bed."

House, vehicle, barn, horse. Yes, he sees Linda's horse standing free and nonchalant, sees the swish of her mangy tail, hears a cheerful, liberated little whinny. The garden is not fenced, and the horse is in it, feeding. Hannibal thinks what there must be, this late in July: tender beets, carrots, bolting lettuce, the very last peas.

"Pickins' are good." He titters, liking the idea that the horse will get a chance to do some damage before he, Hannibal, figures out what to do.

Because he, Hannibal, has not figured out what to do, beyond making it to the other side of the road, which he has already accomplished. A wild notion of lassoing the horse comes to mind. But this is no wild horse, and he's no Bill Hickock. What he *could* do is walk right to it, stroke its neck, talk to it gently, yank up some carrots to have in hand, and lead it back, one carrot at a time. That's one choice. Or he could get behind it and kind of shoo it along, herd it home. That's another. Or he could clap his hands, scream bloody murder, and watch it run to kingdom come. He doesn't know which it will be.

"You can lead a horse to water but you can't make it think," says Hannibal. He chuckles. Suddenly he's having a good time. He's just a little drunk, he's all wrapped up, invisible, in the humid night air, the horse has run free and he has run free and they're having a good time over here at the Lardners' and Sheldon doesn't have a clue.

He walks slowly, stealthily, across the driveway toward the garden, sliding on loose gravel, which grates harshly into the silence. "You oughtta get it paved, Sheldon," he says sternly. Then he burps. He creeps closer to the horse, murmuring, "Dandelion. Atta boy, Dandelion." It strikes him what a trite, stupid name his daughter has bestowed upon this beast. Ah, well, this *is*, after all, a trite, stupid beast. And he tries not to think it, though he just set himself up to think it: what a trite, stupid daughter she is, too. He fights off the shudder of knowledge that for the past twenty years has taken hold of him whenever he's not careful—like a thick clutch of brambles snagging him by the shirt. If he moves, if he so much as breathes, the thorns will rip into his flesh. A good drink usually fends it off, this knowledge, letting him wriggle out of the shirt before the brambles dig in. But now he's stuck out here without a drink, only the last effects of rot-gut, and only a few swigs at that, and he knows what he knows: his children have not gone right. Not that they've gone *wrong* exactly, and not that they're criminals, though Stanley has had his brushes with the law—and Hannibal snorts back a giddy little hoot that rises in his throat, remembering the barn, and pushes away as successfully as always all thought of Stanley's talk of war, which Hannibal has never once let in—but they lack *spunk*.

He bends to pick carrots, because something in him by itself has decided that's how he'll lead the horse away. Just a couple of feet of carrot row will do the trick. Spunk, yes, but there are better words.

Drive, imagination, ingenuity. "*Yankee* ingenuity," he says out loud. All the things *he* might have had once, too, had actually started out having once, too. Shit. Alas, the waste, he thinks, at once mocking himself and hating himself for it. But, as he holds out and admires the bunch of shapely little carrots—and maybe they're not such dummies after all, these Lardners, they can at least grow a carrot—his heart takes a nosedive at the thought of dull pasty Linda and her Jehovah's Witnesses, her dull, mute, pasty, fatherless kid, her Dandelion horse. What *else* might have been? he wonders. W*hat else?* He's just about to let himself follow that question—leading out like a frayed old rope up, up, up from his deep well of disappointment, out beyond its lid of whiskeyed forgetting—

When Sheldon, stumbling out of bed from a deep sleep (though Patty still lies there, totally awake, it's not *her* idea to go to bed at eight, she's chewing over all the things he did wrong during the day, all the things the children did wrong during the day, and while listening to Sheldon shuffling around she knows she'll probably have a doozie of another wrong thing any second now) Sheldon leans his .22 out the window, not really thinking clearly, no, not really thinking *at all* about what he's shooting at out there, whatever it is that he can hear chewing and grunting and strutting around, damn it, decimating his garden, maybe deer, moose, horse, whatever it is, he's got *some*thing in his sites, *he'll* show *it*, and he squeezes the trigger.

• • •

And then, by the time I've heard everyone's version of events, I piece together what happened with Stanley right after, too, after he nearly comes to blows with the State Police, who Patty called first along with an ambulance. And when he gets back from the hospital and Sheldon and Patty come back from the police station to the house, *Hannibal's* house, he won't talk to them. His sister lets them in but he turns abruptly from them, doing them a favor by not spitting at them or strangling them, and goes into another room and slams the door, which for all of Stanley's life never has closed tight and yawns back open right away, so it is only the thudding sound that separates him from those others. And once they are gone and Linda and Kim are in bed, and once he has downed two six-packs, he finally goes for his own gun. He loads it. He bolts out the door and is crossing the road on his way to blow Sheldon's head off, when Everett the old blacksmith drives along, just then exactly, in the last mile of a very long return from his sister's in Pennsylvania. Later, Everett will not be able to remember any other time in the last twenty years he has been out in his vehicle at 3:30 in the morning, but there he is. He stops the pick-up, jumps out, and restrains Stanley without too much trouble because Stanley is dead drunk. Everett grabs the gun, hides it in his own truck, walks him back into the house, and sits with him there all the rest of the night, talking. A man of mostly no words, Everett roots around and slowly pulls enough of them together to talk Stanley through the night and get him safely to the other side. He tells him about birthing two sets of twin sheep at his sister's, the one set blind. He tells him about the winter of '55. He tells him about a forge he once worked at in Millinocket. He tells him about a woman he met when he made a fancy iron fence in Waterville. He tells him about the pole beans that wound their way high up into the tree like in Jack and the Beanstalk and reseeded themselves the next year. He tells him about the buck he bagged last year, and the one the year before, and the one the year before that. He tells him about every mile along a stretch of New Jersey Turnpike when it was raining cats and dogs. He tells him the whole convoluted story of the two Perry Mason reruns he saw in Pennsylvania. It's all he can think to do, besides punch the guy's lights out, and it works. Stanley nods off at seven and sleeps for awhile. He never does ambush Sheldon.

• • •

"Stand over *there*," Rob yelled at me, pointing to the side of the garden with the butt of the rifle.

"*Don't* shoot it in the *garden!*" I yelled back.

"*Damn it!* I'm gonna get the bastard! Now *move!*"

I wasn't really close to the porcupine. It was in the middle of a

jungle of squash vines, while I was way over by the cabbages.
"Let it *eat* the goddamned squash!" I shouted.
"No!"
"I'm sick of all the *shooting!*" I screamed.
"Then get *inside!*" he screamed louder.
"Noooo!" I howled. There were no bounds. No one was listening. No one could see. We could have done anything to each other, no one would have known.
Bang! The shot rang out.
"*Damn you!*" I stood shaking. There was a tremor in the squash leaves, a disturbance that started at one end of the row and moved along it, leaves flopping around as the porcupine crept out.
Bang! He shot again. A cluster of leaves jumped and disintegrated just at the edge of the garden. The porcupine wallowed out and rushed into the woods.
"*I hate you!*" I screamed.
Rob still had the rifle poised on his shoulder when he turned towards me. I waited for him to shoot. It could come to this, and no one would know.
"*You jerk!*" he yelled, then he stomped off into the house.

The quills were everywhere. One by one I picked them up. Pick-up-sticks that lodged in my fingers; I yanked them out. My thumbs were all bloody, but still I picked quills from under the vines and from the flesh of squashes and even from between the withered rows of corn. I sat on the damp ground. A quill went into my thigh. I kept picking up quills.
"It's getting dark," said Rob, appearing suddenly.
"So what," I answered.
"You must be cold."
"So what."
He sighed. Another quill slid into my finger; I pulled it out.
"It wasn't me who shot Hannibal," he said.
"What's that got to do with it?" I replied.
"Look at me, please," he said.
I looked up at him. His face was gray and sad and drained.

"It's got everything to do with it," he said gently.

"It's over," I blurted, in a rush of tears.

"He's dead, Sonia," Rob said. "So cry if you have to." He walked away.

I sat in the squash vines and cried.

• • •

"Will you please leave that thing outside?" I said to Stanley.

"I'm not gonna shoot you."

"Just, please, leave it outside."

He took the gun apart and came in with the pieces in his hand. The house was warm and smelled of cinnamon and wood smoke. Rob pointed to a chair. Stanley sat down. I poured coffee.

Stanley said quietly, "I got a new girlfriend." He looked at me with a dull look I couldn't read. He wasn't trying to get my goat.

"Is she of age?" I asked, not knowing if I could still joke with him.

"You're so mean," he said. I held my breath. He gulped down coffee, then looked at me again, this time his eyes brighter, one of his old snarls starting to bend his lips. I breathed again. "Shit. She's no jailbait. I'd like to bring her around some day."

"Sure. Any time." I drank coffee. For a while we didn't talk.

Finally Stanley said, "I'm goin' down to New Hampshire to look for work. They say there's more construction jobs there, I'll have better luck."

Rob and I both nodded. Rob said, "It'd be good for you to get away from here."

"Yeah," I said.

"Yeah," said Stanley.

We finished our coffee. I said, "We've got this buck hanging around, saw him about an hour ago."

Stanley's eyes widened. We had never told anyone about our deer before. Rob said, "One hell of a big one. Here." He went to the window and showed Stanley where the tracks in the snow circled around the stubs of brussels sprouts and branched off from the garden. Stanley went out and followed the tracks into the woods. I never saw him again.

Later his younger brother came along, looking just like him, angry that they'd been separated.

"He went thatta way," I said, showing him the tracks of deer and man.

The kid juggled his rifle around while he put back on his gloves.

"Careful with that thing," I said.

"Yeah." He scowled. And off he went in Stanley's tracks.

• • •

I walked down the road. The first light coating of snow had fallen and formed a thin crust on the mud and thatch of leaves. Wiggle loped along at my heel, her nose probing every crevice. At last she caught a scent and was off, up the hillside and into the woods. Soon I heard the high-pitched *yip-yip-yip* that was her rabbit-hunting call. As she got closer to the prey, or as she believed she did, the sound took on a eerie, mournful density and depth, and Wiggle became an other-worldly creature, lost in the hunt.

I stopped and listened. Closer, there was a light rustling in the leaves and a brown and white rabbit came bounding through the woods, over the ditch, across the road, and into the dense brush on the other side, its ears stretched back in flight. In three hops it had vanished. I heard Wiggle in hot pursuit, still on the hillside. A minute passed, then another, punctuated by those mournful yips. I waited three minutes more. Finally there was a scramble in the woods, Wiggle landed in the ditch, climbed up, and, panting heavily, her tongue hanging out, she picked up what was left of the rabbit's scent, trotted along to the other side of the road, gave one glance back at me, and vanished into the underbrush, the unflagging *yip-yip-yip* of blissful, futile longing trailing after her.

• • •

It is nearly the end of deer season when I am packing to leave. For good. A jeep pulls right up to the house and we say, screw those hunters. But it's townspeople, neighbors, two older couples. So I kick the suitcases under the bed, push the boxes of pots and pans back into the pantry, and hide all evidence of my departure. We're not telling. We can't explain.

The visitors enter merrily, their glasses steaming up in our warmth. We have been in this house for four years, and they have finally come to pay a call. We joke about this. They sit down gingerly, wary as they take stock of the house, but because it is so much more than they ever expected, all the way back here, they can admire it without reservation, unbutton their wool jackets, and relax. They drink coffee with us. Rob and I are such a pleasant couple. We tell them all the funny little anecdotes about the place, the cute stuff: the dog and bunny rabbit stories, the day Rob went down the well, the truck from Massachusetts that sank in the mud. We are utterly charming. They are thinking, what nice young people after all. It will be months before they find out I've left. I talk to the women about winter, about being alone long hours of the day, about getting through it. Their faces are framed by a hard, steely endurance that I have begun to feel taking hold of my own jaws. They are fat, these women; they have their sicknesses, too; but they do not get killed or kill themselves like the men do. Their duty is to outlive. They bustle with their stoves, fill up town halls with town suppers, spoil their children, remember what needs remembering, and work. They work extraordinarily hard, and they get through. I have a flicker of guilt, not for deceiving them right now, but for not enduring another of their winters.

For an hour we are all pleasant. On their way out they insist we have our picture taken with their brand new color Polaroid. Rob and I, the women, and one of the men huddle together outside the house, and with the season's last golden oak leaves as our backdrop, we are snapped. The happy homesteaders and our neighbors. They give us the picture; I take it with me when I go.

THE STORY

IT WAS AS A WONDERFUL STORY. Abby had been telling me about these people for years, always a little smug when they did something wrong. The things they did got worse and worse. What finally happened was almost too bad to be true.

"There's your story," I'd say to Abby, a writer of some promise but little output, just like me (back then in the eighties and ever after). Her skill was frittered away editing the local weekly, mine, by teaching junior high school English. "Grab that story," I urged her. "It's a winner." But she responded with her usual "Eh," and went back to the chocolate mousse or lobster bisque or whatever gourmet perfection she was whipping up back there in the sticks that day.

The story started this way: The guy was a lawyer in one of those small, depressed Maine coastal towns where once had flourished canneries and fisheries, but now almost nothing was left. His name was Bert, a sluggish man, whose father was also a lawyer. The father, Abby said, had pink flamingos and turquoise birdbaths out on his front lawn. "He's got a Puerto Rican lawn over there on Turtle Hill Road," she said.

Bert did divorces, family disputes, and his neighbors' criminal cases, just as Abby's husband Tom did. In fact, Tom had been in partnership with Bert several years earlier. Now he was on his own. Lawyers have steady work in this neck of the woods, where the winters go on forever and, come April, minds tend to snap and life looks pretty cheap. You can't say it's one particular thing or another, that there's mud instead of blossoms or cold instead of warmth, or that the mill isn't buying wood this year or the payments are overdue on the pickup. But a lot of booze gets drunk. Despair grows thick as fog. And people shoot one another all the time.

I was in that part of Maine for five years before I moved to a snugger corner of the state, right after Janet Parker down the road gave it to her rotten brother in the back of the head with a .22. It was Tom who defended her. She was sent down to Thomaston, but I heard she got out, after seven years, and was doing paste-up at the paper.

Bert had a wife named Bertha; "Bert and Bertha" is what you had to call them. She was a reporter for Abby's paper and, like Abby and me, an aspiring writer. But Bertha's writing was lousy. Her news stories, sensational enough, always missed the point. They lacked control, just as Bertha herself did. She was sloppy and fat and had a kid who got high on sugar and could turn a two-story house upside down in five minutes flat. Control was Abby's theme; excess was Bertha's. Abby battled to maintain her svelte figure, even as she churned out gourmet dinners, while Bertha continued to enlarge.

Bert did his divorces, quarrels, wills, and an annual murder trial, but more and more he took on trust-fund jobs and money in escrow. The local merchants remarked that his checks had begun to bounce, Abby told me. Bert got fatter and pastier in the face, as if the good life had set in a little too hard. The pharmacist started to tell people that Bert had a minor drug habit. The liquor store owner started to tell people Bert had a minor alcohol habit. Even so, life went on pretty much the same. Bertha wrote her bad stories, the kid raced around in a hyperactive whirl, and Bert handled a lot of other people's money.

Did the rest of the story have to happen? I don't know, but it did. Temptation won. Instead of holding the money in trust, investing it where folks requested, Bert took it for himself. He bought booze, drugs, trips to no place in particular, some ugly ornaments for the house, and a few lavish parties, which Abby swore were ruined by Miracle Whip instead of mayonnaise in the lobster salad—all to the tune of $400,000. Bert was caught red-handed.

"Write it!" I told Abby. "He gave you a story. So take it!"

"Eh," she said apathetically. "Let's see what happens." On the phone I heard her food processor whizzing in the background. "Tom's very relieved that Bert's shenanigans are over," she added. "At least he had nothing to do with that creep for the last three years."

But Bert's shenanigans weren't over. A few weeks later, when the kid was staying at his grandparents' and Bertha was sound asleep, the house burst into flames. Bert shot out the back door and barreled down the hill, about as fast as you'd expect someone his size and in his shape to barrel, to find a neighbor's phone. When the volunteers got there, the house was falling down and Bertha was dodging flying embers in the driveway.

"You didn't even wake me! You wanted me to fry!" were Bertha's words, which Abby reported back to me. "Oh was she mad, stomping around out there in her nightie. It was polyester!" Abby gloated.

Now, Bert probably could have struck a deal with the district attorney—everyone figured he still had enough family connections to make use of so he wouldn't have to do a lot of time in the clink—but he panicked. Two days before the larceny indictment was handed down, he fled with Bertha and the kid across the Canadian border into Saint Andrews.

"Tacky!" said Abby, the next time we got together, licking the last creamy globs of a pâté from her thumb. We were in a French restaurant near my new place further down the coast; she had come on one of her two-day visits, which were getting more and more frequent, "just to get away from home." Nothing was wrong there, she maintained. But after a couple of straight bourbons she admitted that Tom was going to more and more Rotary meetings and town suppers and dirt-bike races and other things she'd never in a million years be caught dead at.

"Bert and Bertha escaped, but there was a catch," she said. "When Bert went to close out his bank account before they fled, he discovered that the insurance money, which should have cleared by then, had not. It took another day. So the next day he came *back* to the States, cashed in the money, crossed into Canada again, and met up with Bertha and the brat at the Star-Brite Motel. Nobody got him at the border, though he sure gave them plenty of chances. And the next day they had tickets for Antigua." Abby sipped her drink and looked longingly at the coquilles St. Jacques, which were set before her. Then she giggled.

"Another catch?"

She grinned. "Picture Bertha, while Bert was out crossing borders: in this two-bit motel with the Utrillo prints and stained sheets, watching daytime TV—*Canadian* daytime TV, for God's sake—trying to keep the kid quiet. Eating potato chips and malted milk balls. Bored to death, she called her parents and blurted out where she was hiding. Maybe it was no accident—she knew her parents hated him. And it must have been eating away at her, him running from the house while she was about to smolder in the bed."

"The parents called the cops?"

Abby dabbed at her cream sauce with a piece of baguette. "You got it. In the middle of the night a dozen Canadian Mounties swooped down on the Star-Brite and caught Bertha in her polyester nightie. Now Bert's in Thomaston. Not much chance of bargaining *now*."

"Take this goddamn story, Abby," I said, "and *write it!*"

She dangled a scallop on the end of her fork. "Naah. It's Bertha's story. Let Bertha write it."

Abby sent me clippings to keep me posted as time went on. And I mean *lots* of time. Time for her husband to buy a Jaguar and get an ulcer. Time for Abby to fight with her publisher and quit her job. Time for Bertha to move down to Augusta to be closer to the jail. Visiting Bert one day, she smuggled a file inside a cake and claimed it was a joke.

"He showed the file to the guard right away," Abby said on the phone, "like he didn't have a thing to do with this little stunt. Now they're both in trouble. A joke, can you believe it? She smuggled a file into the jail as a joke!"

"How's Tom taking it?" I asked.

"With Maalox," she said. "And a new television with a screen that covers one side of the house."

"He seems to be on quite a spree these days," I remarked.

"Business must be good," Abby replied without the slightest trace of sarcasm in her voice.

The headline was right up there on the top of the first page of the *Bangor Daily News*: LAWYER HUBBY SHOT BY WIFE. I don't know what made me think Abby had shot Tom, yet when my eyes raced down to find the column, that's what I expected to see. But no, Abby hadn't shot Tom. Bertha had shot Bert, right inside the jail. Even at close range she only managed to nick him in the shoulder.

Abby called. "They can't do *anything* right, these people," she moaned. "By the way," she added, "Tom bought me a diamond bracelet. He's taking me to Hawaii for a couple of weeks, too."

"While you're there," I said, "you ought to write this story. They gave it to you on a silver platter."

"Eh," said Abby. "You know what? *You* can have it."

Abby and Tom may still have been in Hawaii when I read in the paper that Bertha's defense attorney was Tom. I called Abby but got no answer. When I tried a few weeks later, a recording said the number had been changed, and when I asked for the number from Information, I was told it was unlisted. I left several messages for her at Tom's office, but Abby never called me up again.

• • •

So I wrote the story, just as it happened, one-two-three, from Abby's point of view. I'd written other stories, but to get them out had been like pulling teeth, and then nobody ever wanted them. But this one was different: it seemed to write itself. I sent off the manuscript to a classy New York City magazine, *The Brownstone Review*, and in three weeks I got it back. But instead of a regular rejection slip tacked on, there was a letter from the editor:

> It is a pity to see such good writing wasted on such an inflated story, which has little credibility or substance. It strikes me that what you merely *suggest* about the relationship

> between the two attorneys is of far more importance than all the marital squabbles and the rivalries between the supposedly-writing females. I would be interested in seeing your talent at work on worthier material. Try us again sometime.
>
> *Allen R. Davies*, Editor

I was stung. "Supposedly-writing females"! The nerve! I took a knife and stabbed the letter onto my bulletin board as a symbol of all that had gone bad in the literary world.

When I'd cooled down, I told myself to be realistic: maybe this guy knew what works and what doesn't, what sells and what won't. The man was successful, after all; he had to know *something*. And he had said my writing was good and encouraged me to try again. Why hadn't I noticed that in the first place? The man had taste.

So I rewrote the story and told it from the point of view of Abby's husband. Bert didn't burn down the house or go back across the border for his money. My narrator became more and more haunted by his former partner's crimes, filling the story with a growing sense of malaise and fear, but his own behavior never came directly into question. He didn't buy any Jaguars, diamond bracelets, or televisions, or develop any ulcers. I left out the part about smuggling a file in a cake. By the time old Bertha shot Bert in the shoulder, it was inevitable that Tom defend her.

"Better," said Allen R. Davies in his next rejection,

> But you still overdramatize your story, perhaps because this unfortunate attorney is not as corrupt as you'd like to think. The "Bert and Bertha" business is still too <u>cute</u>. I'm not so sure about Bertha anyway. There's nothing worse than writing about writers, don't you agree? You were wise to get rid of the first narrator. And, oh yes, the reference to Puerto Rico is in <u>very</u> poor taste. Do keep trying us.

The lines underneath the *cute* and the *very* were brutally dark and unnecessarily adamant. He'd gotten coffee stains on three pages and lost one page altogether. Still, I thought, if I'm on the right track, I might as well keep going. So I overhauled the story once again. This time, I read up on Republican versions of Watergate and tried to ease myself into a frame of mind through which I could perceive criminal acts in a more charitable light. The story became increasingly psychological; my narrator edged closer and closer to despair. In this approach there was not much room for writers and wives.

Davies took two months to return the manuscript.

> This is becoming a very good story. Given the purer and more intense line of thought, however, your sentences now appear a bit cumbersome. The plot as well as the verbiage could still do with some streamlining. Do try us again.
> Cordially,
> *Allen R. Davies*, Editor

It happened that I was about to embark on a vacation in New York City. I grabbed my story and this latest commentary and stuffed them in my luggage.

What a shock, to be browsing in B. Dalton's and to come across a brand-new, hot-off-the-press book by Allen R. Davies: *The Thinking Gourmet: A Kitchen Guide for the Intelligent Taste*. I needed a few minutes to get it straight: he had written a cookbook. It sold for $21.95. The type was large. Each recipe was introduced by a few lines of Davies' poetry and occupied at least two pages. The recipes called for a lot of fresh goat cheese, porcini mushrooms, arugula, and Szechwan black-bean paste—things you didn't see very often in Maine in those days, though I suppose Abby came up with them when she had to. I put the book back on the shelf. But then, later the same day, as I browsed in the Gotham Book Mart, I happened upon a notice of a reading at a church in the Village featuring a Czechoslovakian writer in exile, Milan Hracnic, and his American promoter, none other than Allen R. Davies. They would both be reading from their latest works.

I counted nineteen people inside that church, including the two poets and Nadia Trelinger, whom I recognized instantly from a recent photo in the *Book Review*; she was there to introduce the two others. The tall, lanky, gray-haired one in blue jeans was easy to peg as Allen R. Davies; the short one with the wispy beard and heavily framed glasses, wearing a greasy suit, had to be Milan Hracnic. The program said that Hracnic was one of the most respected poets of Czechoslovakia, though his work was banned in his own country. He had flourished during the glorious burst of free expression permitted just before, then squelched by, the Soviet invasion of 1968. For ten years he stayed on in Prague, emptying bedpans in a clinic. In 1979 he fled to the south of France, where he had been living ever since.

Nadia Trelinger arose, wearing a straight-cut suit of huge black-and-white checks and looking all of her seventy-odd years, though she was clearly made up to seem fifty. She read verbatim from the biography in the program, from the first word to the last, never looking up, throwing in not so much as a word of her own literary wit and wisdom. She read, her face expressionless: a giant, blank, human chessboard. I blushed for her, but no one else seemed perturbed.

And then, to my consternation, the tall, lanky fellow in blue jeans arose to speak for the freedom of the oppressed Czechs. Reading the English translation of his own poems in a deep monotone, he evoked countless images of Soviet tyranny, Soviets swarming like ants, descending like arctic snowfalls, oozing like lava from an angry volcano. A video recorder buzzed from the balcony, right until Hracnic's last words. Following Nadia Trelinger's lead, all eighteen of us rose to our feet in an ovation.

This left the short man with the wispy beard, dark-rimmed glasses, and greasy suit to be Allen R. Davies. Nadia managed a few improvised words for her friend, and together they struggled to lower the microphone to the level of his mouth, which was several inches below hers. Once this was accomplished, the sound lost, the sound regained, the shrill electronic hum controlled, Davies announced that he would read first from last year's volume, *High Plains Holo-*

caust Express*, and then from his most recent work, *The Thinking Gourmet*. And he began with an elegy to a youth who had died of AIDS and ended with his recipe for Crispy Peking Duck. The audience applauded politely.

Afterwards, I took a deep breath, made my way to the altar, and waited while a young woman in sequined boots nodded earnestly as Davies signed a copy of his cookbook. He smiled at me; I introduced myself. The sensitivity in his eyes turned to stony blankness. I repeated my name. "From the story," I added, "the story in Maine. That I keep sending."

"Oh!" he exclaimed, recognition brightening his face. His smile returned, sweetened, welcomed, and broadened, revealing small gray teeth. He grabbed my hand and shook it.

I fumbled for something to say. "I particularly liked your reading of Wild Mushrooms Stroganoff," I said.

"I am *so* pleased," he replied with such sincerity in his voice that I found myself blushing. "Listen," he said, "after I'm through with this"— and he fluttered his short little arms in circles around the famed Czech freedom poet and a small entourage of fans, as if they were no more than a few odd insects to be dispensed with— "would you do me the honor of meeting for a drink? I'd like to talk with you." There was no questioning his sincerity. We agreed to meet at the Peacock Café in two hours.

In the café, I slid over on the wooden bench to make room for him.

"*You*," he said emphatically, setting down my glass of wine and his glass of something green, "are a *very* promising writer." I could picture just how hard he was underlining the *very* as he said it. His wide grin was part boyish and charming, part sickly. "And you must persevere," he added. "Don't get discouraged."

"Not even by you?" I asked.

An intensely wounded expression swept across his features. "Do you think I give this assistance to *everyone*? Believe me, I wouldn't spend the time on your work that I do if I didn't believe it had enormous originality and potential. I have *discovered* some important talent, you know." He hunched over his drink, his shoulders narrowing to a thin, double hump out of which arose the bespectacled face on barely a neck at all. "Look, you know as well as I do, some things in this world have value." He searched my eyes for agreement; I nodded. "Some things don't." I nodded again.

"Take this Hracnic," he said, and leaned back more casually, fingering the wispy beard. Suddenly he burst out laughing, then—just as suddenly—stopped. "I went to see him in France three years ago, after being deeply touched by his poetry. *You'll* appreciate this," he said in a low, confiding voice, as if he knew me very well. He hunched forward again. "I had been writing then on the oppression of Jewish intellectuals by the Soviets, and his work struck such a chord! It seemed to contain the original meaning of freedom, an empathy for all the world's oppressed." He paused, waiting for a sign of understanding.

"I see," I said.

"You know," he went on, "whatever was purest and most essential in the original Bolshevik movements, before the unspeakable contamination, well, that purity was in Hracnic, in his words. He was the soul, I think you could say, of pure revolution." Davies spoke these words with passion.

He lifted his drink and took a perfunctory sip. "Hracnic was something of a mission for me. First, learning Czech well enough to do the translations. Then, making contact with him by letter and convincing him that I, and my interest, were authentic. After we'd agreed on a visit, I had to locate the little village in the south of France, arrive there by the most arduous series of trains and buses, and finally make my way up the dirt road to his cottage—which I chose to do by foot. Nine miles."

Davies paused so I could savor the unwavering devotion and effort that went into this odyssey. I smiled. He smiled.

"And then, what did I find? Not the ancient, broken stone cottage in the wilderness that I expected, but a villa of the most luxurious order. Servants brought us drinks by the swimming pool. Three Algerian groundskeepers maintained a rose garden worthy of Versailles. I met Hracnic's wife only when he gave me the tour of the mansion; she was bending over a stove in a sweltering kitchen. And during the whole day—yes, he gave me a whole day!—he spoke of nothing but the suffering of his people, the banning of the works of the important writers, his visions of liberation and justice."

"The hypocrite!" I exclaimed.

"But NO!"

I thought Davies would leap up on the table like a monkey, so strongly did his little body rock forward with tremors of protest.

"No, Oh God, NO! Can't you *see!*" He gulped down the rest of whatever it was that smelled of licorice. "Oh, you with your black-and-white view of things, your absolutes. They're *hackneyed*, I tell you. They have no place in dealing with *evil* in this world as it has evolved, now, in this century. This man Hracnic, living under the menace that he has, has outsmarted *your* absolutes." He grinned again, that same boyish, sickish, but charming grin.

I felt as stung as I had by his first letter of rejection, and I waited in hurt silence for him to continue with an explanation. Only when he turned, ordered more drinks, and faced me with a smile, did I realize that what he had just said had *been* the explanation.

"On that momentous day," Davis continued, "Hracnic showed me a story he had written."

The waitress interrupted, setting down the drinks. Davies made a sweeping gesture for the check, then found he did not have enough money. I paid.

"The central symbol of his story was so compelling, such an irresistible metaphor, that I found it winding its way into my own dreams, my own words. It began with a lion bursting out of the jungle and traveling continents to America—in fact, to Houston, Texas—in search of its mate, which had been taken into captivity. This lion somehow took possession of *me*. I swear, I could see nothing but this fierce, proud animal roaming the universe, roaming the paths of my own invention." He smiled inwardly at himself, pleased with his choice of words. "And I wrote a long poem, undoubtedly the best thing I have ever written, using Hracnic's metaphor." Slowly he sipped the foul licorice drink, waiting for my response.

"That's quite amazing," I said at last.

"But DON'T you even want to know WHERE IT IS?" he exploded angrily. "My POEM? My BEST poem?"

I wiped away the spittle that had flown onto my face. "Where is it?" I asked quietly.

"Waiting, as his story is waiting. He refuses to publish his story, in any country or in any language—God knows, *I'd* be dying to publish it!—while the Soviets still control his country's government. This waiting is his protest." He took a sip. "This is his integrity." Davies finished off his second glass. "This is his *life*, damn it!"

"I see," I repeated.

"And how could *I* possibly bring out a poem based on his metaphor, telling a story in the same vein, before *his* story is published? Can't you see? *Mine* has to come after his. There is no other way." He crushed his small plastic straw in his clammy hand. "My future depends on the course of history, the showdown between liberty and tyranny!"

We sat silently for a few moments as he let his sadness, and the significance of its cause, settle over us.

Finally I said, "That's a great story."

He looked at me, first stunned, then with a storm brewing in his eyes. "But I didn't even *tell* you the story."

"I mean the story *about* the story." I held tightly onto my chair, awaiting the torrent of anger.

"Oh God," he moaned, cupping his hands over the top of his head. "You *would* say that." He mumbled the words that were meant for me softly down into his own chest.

I figured that was the end of it; I was a hopeless ignoramus and he would make short shrift of the rest of this disastrous encounter. But I was wrong. He did some literary small talk, we had another drink, and he invited me home with him. What the hell, I thought; maybe my story still had a chance, after all. So I went back to his walk-up on the Upper West Side and I slept with him.

As I was leaving the next morning, he sat at the kitchen table, wrapped snugly in his ex-wife's kimono. "You know," he said, "I was thinking, last night. It might be better if you took that story out of Maine altogether. That backwoods angle, I don't know. It strikes me as somewhat overblown."

• • •

Eventually there were no women in my story, there were no writers and no crooks and no Puerto Ricans, either. It took place in New York City, in the present tense, and no sentence contained more than nine words. It evolved into one lawyer's meditation on guilt and innocence as he witnessed the slow downfall of a colleague who was misled into doing insider trading on the stock exchange.

"This is excellent work," Allen R. Davies wrote back.

> Still, I've made a few suggestions. I know you have no illusions that any intimacy between us can influence the outcome of my magazine's decision on this piece. But feel free to try us again.
>
> Cordially,
> A.R.D.

The story was covered in blue pencil marks. None of the plot or action of the story had been changed, but just about all the words had been. I retyped the story using Allen R. Davies' words, and I sent it back to him.

Three months later he accepted the story for publication, and so began my career as a writer. Within the year the story was snapped up for the O. Henry Awards and two other anthologies. One editor hailed the use of the stock exchange as "the perfect symbol of the ambiguous moral landscape of our time."

With this success, it was not difficult gaining entry into the better Eastern artists' colonies where, thanks to my simple country manners and my willingness to let others have my Sunday breakfast bacon, I made many friends. I won grants and was able to stop teaching English. My new friends found me positions in summer writing workshops. One who took pride in her powerful connections got three big-shot moviemakers to read my story. A Hollywood producer made me an offer.

"My only objection," he said, "is that there are no women in this story."

I almost blurted out that there had once been. Then I thought of poor old Bertha, finding her place on the stock exchange, and I bit my tongue. "But there can't possibly be," I replied.

He paid me a fortune for the movie rights and for consulting on the screenplay.

I've written nothing for the last several years. Between grants and the movie, I'm well set up for a long, long time. But I did make use of one blissful summer stint at the MacDowell Colony to begin a novel. It's about an elephant that breaks loose from the jungles of Africa to prowl the world in search of his mate, who had been taken into captivity. These thirty pages have become my work-in-progress, which accompanied a number of applications and got me a huge advance. It's such a promising beginning that the ending barely matters. Readers tell me they find the central image irresistible.

JOSEPHINE'S RELEASE

"JOSEPHINE! OH JOSEPHINE!"

Only after she shut off the vacuum cleaner did Josephine hear Doris's calls. They became shriller—"Jo-oh-sephine"—and more insistent—"Jo-sephine!"

She went to the hallway and leaned over the banister. "I'm in the bedroom!" She knew very well that with the door closed, two flights down, Doris would not hear her.

"Josephine! I need you!"

Josephine loaded more things into the laundry basket from the mess piled on the floor. She found wet towels on the bed, underthings tossed everywhere—she flung them all in.

"Josephine!"

She filled the basket and took it downstairs, balanced on her hip under one long, slender arm—not on her head, as she might have done in the streets of Port-au-Prince, as her mother had done, baskets of mangoes held high atop that proud head, arms swaying, hips swaying, a big-boned woman who had sold fruit at the market to put Josephine through school. So Josephine could have a better life. A better life!

"*Josephine!*"

"I am *coming!*" Josephine called out. She set the laundry basket on the kitchen counter, then descended one more flight and barged into the cluttered office without knocking.

Doris looked up from her nest of papers and smiled, her lower lip rigid, a sure sign of doing battle with a scowl. This new haircut of hers, thought Josephine, was even shorter than the last one; why didn't Doris just shave her head? Her face seemed paler and fatter now. And all that black didn't help: the black sweatshirt and those ballooning black harem pants. Like clown pants. How could she bear so much cloth around her in Brooklyn's suffocating summer weather? Besides, those pants should have been in the laundry basket long ago.

"What is it?" Josephine asked. "Are you ill?"

"I need tea," said Doris. "And a sandwich. Where were you?"

"I was in your room, cleaning up your things, getting ready to do your laundry, because you asked me to." Josephine was precise with her English; she had mastered the language deliberately, like a weapon. "And I do not *run* down the stairs."

"Okay, Jo, so take it easy."

"And all this fuss for lunch?"

"I'm in the middle of this essay again, Jo, and I can't stop. You remember—the post-colonial feminism talk I gave at Columbia last year? I've rewritten it a hundred times." Doris forced another half-smile, shrugged, and made her eyes get big and helpless. Even her son Jacob didn't resort to such devices when he wanted his way! "Be a dear, Josephine. Tuna fish would be fine."

"I'll bring it when it's ready," said Josephine, the broad bones of her face setting themselves in a hard, resolute line. She no longer boiled over with anger as she had so often during her first years in New York. Now she maintained a slow, proud, steady simmer.

"When it's ready," she repeated. "I'll bring it. There is no more need to yell." Slowly she moved around the room to pick up the morning's accumulated cups and plates. There were dark brown tea stains on the desk, encrusted circles that would take so much scrubbing. More rings made a shabby pattern on the oak bookcase that used to be so nice.

"And watch for Jacob, please, Josephine?" said Doris with that girlish, pleading upturn on the "please." "His father said he'd bring him back by one this afternoon."

Josephine snorted.

Doris said, "I told him, very firmly this time, that if he wasn't on time, right on the dot, I'm not kidding, he could forget next week."

Josephine snorted again, fitting the last mug onto her fingertips. And what would *you* do with Jacob if you had him all weekend? she thought. Turn him over to *me*? She closed the door with the tap of her foot, just as Doris called out, in that most urgent of tones, "Rye bread, Josephine! Rye!"

"Patience, Josephine, patience," said the lawyer each time she called to remind him she had been here long enough; her papers had been in order months ago, her sponsor's papers, too. Doris had held the key to her freedom for the four years Josephine worked in this house. To get a green card she had only to stay with the same employer and put in the correct amount of time. And now there was only the wait for the papers to go through, the final ruling—a few months is what the lawyer had said a few months ago; a few months was what he said last week—a few months forever while the papers made the slow circuit from desk to desk, to someone with a stamp, someone else with a signature, someone else with a sigh. "Ahump." "Yes." "No." "Yes." A few more months, the rest of the lawyer's fees, that was all, and then Josephine could leave this job, could leave *this*...

It was Saturday. She couldn't call the lawyer.

Josephine drained the liquid from the can and mashed the fish with the back of a fork in hard, rapid pushes. She shook a big blob of mayonnaise from a spoon, threw in some slivers of chopped onion, and mounded it all on the rye. The kitchen clock ticked off the seconds. A window closed in the house next door; the whirring of an air conditioner started. The sandwich done, Josephine sat for a moment on a stool beside the counter, relieved by the quiet that was the absence of commands, annoyed by the quiet that was the absence of life. She sighed, got up, put the lunch on a tray.

A few minutes later, as she set the tray down on the desk, she noticed the stack of new mail on the shelf behind Doris, and in it the pale, air-mail blue.

"Well, what?" asked Doris, looking up again from her scribbled page. When the typist wouldn't come on Saturday, Doris became more frazzled as the day wore on. "What are you waiting for?"

"I thought I saw today's mail and I'd like mine, please."

Doris blew out an enormously long sigh. She turned and reached for the pile of envelopes, and though it was obvious which belonged to Josephine, she began to peruse them, one by one.

"Ah, finally, the honorarium check from the Radcliffe conference. Hmmm...an invitation to some library shindig...Oh hell, I told the electrician *not* to send a bill until he redid the mess he made in the kitchen, and *look!*" She mused silently over other pieces. And then there was the pale blue.

She held it up as if to see it better. "Henrietta. Is that your oldest one?"

"No, she's my youngest. I showed you the new pictures last week." Josephine could not keep the irritation out of her voice.

"How sweet, that the baby writes you."

The baby! The "baby" was nearly eight years old now, and Dani was ten. Josephine had not seen her girls in four years.

Slowly, Doris proffered the envelope. Slowly, Josephine lifted her hand to take it. But just as she felt the soft paper firmly locked between her own thick palm and thumb, she saw from the expression on Doris's face that the game had not ended.

"And look! Two letters in one day! So official-looking, too, when your husband writes on his school's stationery."

Josephine fumed silently. Doris made it sound as if he'd stolen stationery, when he was the principal, the man in charge!

"I can't remember the last time I saw you get a letter from Henry."

"Hen-*ri!*" Josephine burst out.

"Hen-*ri!*" mimicked Doris. With a majestic swoop of her arm, she handed Josephine the envelope.

"Thank you," said Josephine.

"You're welcome," said Doris. "Let me know the minute Jacob gets home."

Josephine finished washing the kitchen floor. She had vacuumed the living room rug, the couch, and the drapes, and was folding laundry in the hallway when the intercom buzzed, summoning her back down to the office. She knocked and went in. Doris had wedged the phone receiver between her shoulder and chin while her hands rummaged wildly in piles of paper, like a dog pawing through earth for buried bones. Josephine began to back out, but Doris pointed to the armchair. "Wait, wait, I'll be right off," she whispered.

Josephine cleared a pile of books off a chair and sat down.

"But sweetie," Doris said into the phone, "They didn't even *ask* me to look at his CV… Um-hum…No, they want it to appear just so, and face it, I'm not on any of those committees… The tenure thing, of course…I don't mind, no…Right, they recognize *him*, too, let's not kid ourselves…Well, it *is* international…uh-huh, instant recognition, uh-huh…" Doris laughed. "Oh, no, I *haven't* heard." Doris put down her papers, leaned all the way back in the big leather chair, and swung her bare feet up on the desk.

Josephine stood and silently mouthed the words, "I'll come back," but Doris shook her head and pointed at the chair. "Relax, Josie," she urged.

"Uh-huh…Uh-huh…Yeah…Well, it doesn't surprise me, after that bogus curriculum meeting…Well, not exactly, but just when I was proving honest-to-God interference, *she* shut me up." Doris lowered her feet, sat back up, and started digging through the papers again.

Josephine, meanwhile, did mental calculations, trying to figure her month's budget in a neatly divided ledger in her head, where columns of numbers expanded and contracted as she moved around her tiny sums. It would never work if she had to pay off the lawyer now. She'd have to cut back somehow, send less to Henri, no clothes for the girls. But school started in a few weeks, they needed things. She'd have to put away less for them here, but the less she put away, the farther off the day they'd come and join her.

"Okay, here it is, I found it…Yeah, this book is killing me…Oh, of course, are you kidding? The most important thing *I've* done? It's the most important thing *anybody's* done." Doris threw back her head and laughed. "Okay, listen." She pushed the receiver against her neck and said in a loud whisper, "You, too, Josie, listen, okay? It's the letter to the *Times*." Doris read out loud in her fast, singsong voice.

Josephine took thirty dollars out of the mental clothes column and put it back into the bank account, then she took twenty dollars from the column for her own winter coat and moved it into the column for the girls. That shrunk the coat money down to fifty again but made one hundred and twenty dollars so far for school. She sighed. She was not going to subject her husband to menial work. Better they stay down there a little longer. When she stopped this job she'd learn data processing, make some real money. There had to be enough to send Henri into courses as soon as he arrived; his first job had to be dignified, in his own profession, otherwise he'd wind up like her, once a teacher, now…this!

"…You with me, Roz? Okay. Here's the end: 'In the face of such global complacency, it is all the more important for us to support the local call for self-determination.'"

Doris smiled at Josephine as she read the last words, while Josephine tried to imagine what self-determination meant to a woman who could not pick up her own soiled underpants from the bedroom floor.

"Yeah, thanks. I think so too…To the *Times*, then copies to Amnesty and the congressmen."

Josephine shifted in the chair. If she were only able to finish sorting laundry, she'd be ready to leave when Jacob came back. It was past two already, and on Saturdays she was supposed to be through at noon. When was the last time she'd left at noon? At least a month ago, maybe two.

"Well?" Doris was asking, the phone hung up. "What do *you* think?"

Josephine was speechless, caught in her inattention.

"The *letter*, Josie, what did you think about the letter?"

"Oh, very good, Doris. It's a very good letter." Josephine bit her tongue and shifted again in the chair. She waited.

"Well, what *is* it, Josie? I *am* trying to work!"

A surge of warmth rose quickly in Josephine's face. "*You* called *me* down here!"

"Oh yes!" Doris laughed. "Would you *please* call Raoul's and find out where he is? Jacob was supposed to be home an hour ago!"

Mid-afternoon descended on this house like a shroud. In the morning, light reached only the top two floors, and even then it had to sneak through in diagonal shafts that seemed to squeeze themselves between the brownstones. Now that brief tease of light had vanished, too. Downstairs, the office was dark as a tomb. Josephine turned lights on everywhere; the bulbs gave out more heat. Even with the air conditioning turned high, the humidity was intense. She felt like the tuna sealed in a can. Windows in this house had not been opened for weeks, and the ceiling fan in the kitchen kept recirculating the same stale, moist air.

Swish, swish... The swish of the fan and the wheeze of the air conditioner were the only sounds. Josephine finished dusting the impossible wicker chairs and went back to the kitchen. She washed her hands, then checked the stew simmering on the stove. When she prodded it with a fork, the meat pulled apart in soft strands. She cut potatoes into chunks and threw them in, then washed and cut green beans, which would go in last.

A hot supper every day, no matter what the weather.

No candy or store-bought cookies.

No toys in the kitchen, no toys in the basement, no toys anywhere on the ground floor. These were the rules.

Never ever disturb Doris in the office: not with Jacob, not with incoming phone calls, not with Raoul, her brothers, or her mother. There was no emergency in this world that couldn't wait until she'd finished working for the day.

These were the rules.

Never sit there doing nothing. There is always something to do.

Do not go back to Flatbush for the night until you've checked with her.

Rules.

Josephine sat at the counter doing nothing for an instant, dreaming of the cold chicken and fruit salad she would have at home, the place she thought of as her real home, the room in Marguerite's apartment where she lived on Saturday nights and Sundays. There, a breeze always came through the kitchen window and licked at the curtains, bringing in the racket of children playing, music from a dozen different radios, men laughing. After supper, Josephine would go out and sit on the stoop with Marguerite and the others. Watching people stroll past, they'd talk late into the night of harvests, riots, escapes, and loves in Gonaïves and Jacmel. She would watch other people's children play in the fire hydrants, staying up long past their bedtimes.

Here, she heard herself breathing, the clock ticking, the slight change in the wheezing of the air conditioner, the bubbling of stew.

She got up and dumped in the green beans. "Fini," she said out loud, startling herself with the sound of her own voice, which suddenly filled the room. She turned the fire off, leaving the steam to cook the beans.

When the bell rang, the house jumped to life. No sooner had Josephine opened the door than chaos erupted: a small dog sprang out of nowhere and began tearing through the living room, its tail whipping wildly. Jacob giggled and shrieked, as out of control as the pup, his shirt soaking wet, shorts coated with mud.

"Jacob! Where have you been? What's that dog…"

"Josephine!" exclaimed Raoul. In one huge, sweeping gesture he handed her a package and hugged her tightly.

Laughing and holding her nose, she pushed him away. "Raoul, you stink. Where have you two been?" She looked him up and down and laughed more. His eyes peered out brightly from the shaggy black hair, which converged in a curly mess with his heavy dark beard. His T-shirt was blotchy with large wet spots and he wore khaki shorts that revealed tremendous furry thighs. And he held onto a lit pipe. Doris would kill them all!

"Prospeck Park!" gasped Jacob. "Piddly jumped into the duck pond and…" Jacob collapsed onto the floor in paroxysms of giggles.

"Piddly!" shrieked Josephine, at a loss as to which potential catastrophe she should attend first. "Get that dog!"

Raoul lunged for the animal as it was clawing the carpet, ready to dig its way under the sofa.

"Don't worry, Josephine, I'm taking it home with me," said Raoul, wrestling the puppy onto his lap. He sat on the carpet, leaned his sweaty back against the sofa, and sprawled out his legs. A big, dirty man, noisy and passionate. Josephine tried to imagine the Doris, a different Doris, who had once married him. Impossible. Growling playfully, the puppy chewed at his wrists. "Piddly will stay at my house for Jacob," he said.

"And learn some manners there, I hope." Josephine retreated quickly to the kitchen and, with trepidation, pressed the buzzer on the intercom. "Jacob is home," she called to Doris, but did not wait for an answer. She grabbed a saucer and set it on the floor beside Raoul. Immediately he dumped ashes from his pipe into it, then began filling the pipe again.

"Raoul! She'll kill us all!"

"Let her!" he said, grinning broadly, as he lit a match.

The puppy sniffed at the saucer, then stepped into it, knocking all the ashes on the rug.

"Piddly did it! Piddly did it!" screeched Jacob, now also on all fours. "Woof! Woof!" he barked. He flung himself onto the armchair and, perched on his knees, sat panting, his hands out in front of him like paws.

"Come here, Jacob, you're getting mud all over the chair!" said Josephine, but Jacob hurled himself onto the floor and rolled over, laughing uncontrollably.

"Play dead, Jacob!" ordered Raoul sternly. Jacob held himself rigid, his face buried in the carpet. "Good dog!" said Raoul.

Taking a deep breath, Josephine sat in the wicker chair. She pulled strands of tape off the package Raoul had brought her and gently unpeeled the paper, careful not to tear it. "Oh, again my favorites, Raoul. You must like to see me getting fat!"

"No, no, you're not a bit fat, and this way you can have them on Sunday with a little peace and quiet."

"Chocolates!" cried Jacob, his voice muffled as he sent the word straight into the rug. He turned his face so his manic bright eyes shone out mischievously at them. "I want chocolate!"

"You are acting like someone who's been eating candy all day long," said Josephine.

"Dead, Jacob, play dead!" commanded Raoul. Jacob hid his face in the rug again. "The chocolates are for Josephine, not you, do you understand?" he said softly. Jacob nodded and Raoul ran his fingers through the boy's hair.

"Did he finish the antibiotic?" asked Josephine.

Raoul nodded, puffing on the pipe. "And his throat looks clear."

"Oh, good."

"The blue T-shirt bit the dust," added Raoul, grinning again. Josephine smiled back. He had taught her "bite the dust" a long while back. He'd once fought as hard as Josephine to get the language and barely even had an accent now, yet they'd always had this bond: they were Doris's foreigners. Now Raoul stroked the puppy, asleep on his lap. Then he turned to Jacob and began to tickle him lightly on the ribs.

Jacob shrieked, rolled over, suddenly sat up, and threw his face into Raoul's, screaming, "Woof! Woof! Woof!" Father and son fell back against the couch in gales of laughter.

"You are both children!" Josephine reprimanded, frowning at the thought of the ever-growing disaster before them. "Two infants!" Then she giggled, too. She looked down into her lap, folded the paper back around the box of chocolates, and pressed the tape at the seams. "Jacob, my dear, you haven't even said hello!"

He trotted over to her on all fours and sat beside her on his knees, whimpering a sad-dog sorry whimper. Then he lifted his front paws onto her knees.

"Poor puppy," she said, and helped him climb up into her lap, where he nestled comfortably. He held tightly to her forearm with one hand. "Poor puppy, how I missed you!" Jacob began to lick her cheek softly. "Oh, that tickles, my sweet." She held his face in her two hands and kissed him on the forehead. Then he nestled in closer and calmed down as they wrapped their arms snugly around each other.

"Are your girls okay?" asked Raoul.

Josephine sighed. "I got a letter from the little one today."

"Henrietta," murmured Jacob sleepily.

"Henrietta," she repeated. "She doesn't like the uniform required in the new school."

"She has to wear a uniform in the third grade?" asked Jacob.

"Yes, in this school in Haiti."

"Yuck. Tell her to come here to school with me."

"Oh yes, Jacob, she would like that. Me, too."

"And everything else?" asked Raoul.

"Normal," said Josephine. "Whatever that means."

The three of them sat in easy silence, Raoul puffing on the pipe, the puppy fast asleep, Jacob nearly asleep himself, Josephine's mind a pleasant blank. And then suddenly the puppy sprang into the air barking.

"Get that dog out of here this minute!" hollered Doris from the doorway. "That dog and that pipe! What is going on here? Look at you!"

"Hello, Doris, my love," said Raoul, getting to his feet. He scooped the puppy up from the floor and let him dangle in the curl of his left arm, paws flailing in midair.

"Don't 'my love' me!" she said. "Look at the smoke in here." She stood with her hands on her big hips, frowning at him. Then she started to cough. "And a dog! You know how allergic I am!"

"We're leaving, we're leaving," said Raoul, his own pique flaring momentarily. "Keep your pants on."

She glowered at him, then turned her angry face to Jacob. She rearranged her features into a welcoming smile, but too late. Josephine could feel his little body tense. She squeezed him gently, intending an invisible caress. But Doris's eyes began to darken again, taking it all in: the tender cuddle, the dirt.

"Jacob," said Doris.

Jacob clutched Josephine more tightly and Doris saw him. Her mouth began to twitch.

Josephine first thought: Let her, let her cry. It serves her right. Unmoved, she watched Doris's face start to collapse: chin fall, eyes puff and redden, nose pinch in. Her lower lip quivered. It would take only one second more. Damn, thought Josephine. She patted

Jacob reassuringly and whispered very softly into his ear, "Go, run to your mother and give her a kiss. Hurry." And she eased him quickly off her lap.

"Jo-oh-sephine!" Doris yelled from the kitchen as Josephine untied her apron. "Monday when you get in, remember, shopping comes first! I see we're nearly out of cereal. And then you'll have to take down the curtains and…"

Click. Josephine pulled the front door shut and stepped from the air-conditioned room into the hush of a stifling summer evening. Brooklyn had become a brownstone rain forest. Rain oozed up from the sidewalks and stoops just as surely as it poured down from the sky. She darted along the street, dodging umbrellas, sidestepping puddles which filled deep crevices in the broken pavement, then bounded down the subway stairs. In the station there was no air, only a dank vacuum. She swabbed rain from her forehead, perspiration from her neck. The clatter of the Brighton train which she'd just missed still echoed between the tile walls.

Across the platform, a white-haired grandfather wearing a tweed jacket sat on a bench and opened his umbrella. She recognized him as a doorman on Grand Army Plaza, once from Cap-Haïtien. He twirled the umbrella along the floor, spinning off rain drops, and sang a Creole song in a deep voice. It was a song from the hillsides, not one she knew. He bent forward stiffly and wiped moisture from the umbrella, caressing it tenderly with a tissue, while the jaunty syncopation of his tune hopped through the tunnel like a stone skipped across the tranquil surface of a cool, clear lake.

Bobbi and Loretta

Loretta shoves a piece of tofu in the sand. She thinks I'm asleep. With her long red thumbnail she drills it down so it's partly buried, then she flicks a piece of clam shell over it. I squint one eye open just enough to see. She takes a drag on her cigarette, rubs out the butt in the sand, and pushes that down, too. Then she closes up the empty plastic salad box and snaps the rubber band back around it, the band sliding from her fingers and encircling the plastic with the screech of a sour violin note. Now her eye is on the hot dog stand, and sooner or later she'll sneak over there. This vegetarian thing's been worse for her than me.

I roll onto my back, my eyes closed tight, or so it seems.

Andy Ferrone comes ambling up from the wet strip of sand with one of his kids in tow. He was a year ahead of us in high school and played baseball like a pro. But now he's got a gut that tumbles out over the drawstring of his trunks, rolls of pale dough punctuated with wiry black hairs. His breasts are starting to swell out, too.

"Hey!" he says to Loretta. "Howzit goin'?" He crouches beside her while the kid circles around us in a sulk. Son or daughter, I can't tell, about eleven, wearing a T-shirt and shorts. Andy's soft, spongy thighs, squatting low over his heels, are too close to my face. Tofu thighs. A little knot of nausea hits me just below the navel.

"Make yourself useful," Loretta says to him, "and oil my back please." She hands him the Johnson's baby stuff and rolls onto her stomach. Her back is one unbroken shade of tan, something between butterscotch and graham cracker. Me, I've still got strap marks from last year.

"That you I seen jogging the other day?" Andy asks, rubbing her back in large, mindless circles.

"Yup. Bobbi and I run two miles, three times a week."

"Didn't see Bobbi. Just you."

"Musta been Saturday. She got a foot cramp that wouldn't stop."

Saturday morning had been cold and windy, and we wore the new sweatsuits from Macy's latest One-Day Sale, Loretta's fuchsia, mine teal. We like to make a good impression: Loretta and I have lived in this neighborhood, a couple of blocks from the beach, for all our lives. That's forty-seven years. But my foot seized up after only a few hundred yards, so I limped back to the boardwalk and sat on a bench, surrounded by Russians wearing honest-to-God coats (this was June, for heaven's sake) and kerchiefs tied under their chins. They sat three or four to a bench, heads up, eyes closed, sunning themselves like seals on rocks. And out there, past the wide empty beach (the tide was low), just before the line where the angriest waves slapped down and spat their muddy foam, out there all alone was Loretta, a solitary fuchsia figure striding against the murky grays that were the sand, ocean, sky, and air of Brighton Beach.

"For Godssakes, Loretta, whatdya need to jog for?" asks Andy now. "You're already in great shape."

Small bones'll do it every time. Since the third grade, no matter how skinny I got (and a few times I did get skinny), I've always felt horsey next to Loretta.

"Naah," she says, "I'm trying to get into shape. So's Bobbi." A pause hangs ominously, and I don't dare open my eyes now. I feel their gazes burning on my midriff, my thighs, the squishy parts of my upper arms and all my other flabby spots, I hear the words, unspoken, saying *she's* the one who *really* needs the exercise. For a moment I am stung by this pause, stung that I, who'd sat on that bench with all the Russians—choking up at the sight of my best friend being so alone, so tough, so brave—stung that I could be the target of such a mean-spirited pause.

But then Loretta says, "Uh-uh. We're in this thing *together*. A whole new routine. We're not getting any younger, in case you didn't notice. So we're off meat too. No steaks, no burgers, no scallopinis for me, no corned beef for her." She sighs wistfully. "We're gonna be healthy, goddamn it, if it kills us."

"You smoke cigarettes," says the kid, who drives the point home by stomping a foot and sending sand into my face.

"Shit!" I cry, as if he has woken me up from a sound sleep. "Who threw sand at me?" I wipe at my eyes and prop myself up on one elbow. Loretta and Andy smile.

Andy laughs, a hollow bellow. "I wouldn't give up meat for nothin'. You girls are crazy."

The kid turns away from us, looks toward the water, and hurls out over his (or her, I still can't tell) shoulder, "Sitting in the sun gives you cancer."

We ignore the kid.

"Smoking, maybe, I can see that," says Andy, shaking his head sadly. "But meat!"

"Animal fat goes straight to your heart," says Loretta, who now believes herself to be an expert, though I'm the one who read the books. "Blocks up all your arteries."

"I know everybody says so," Andy sighs. In our circle, no one rushes onto any bandwagons. "But I'll take my chances." He sighs again. The three of us squint off into the crowd of sunbathers all around.

"Look what happened to Frank Morelli," Andy says. "Young guy our age, in nearly perfect health, and then whammo, dead. So he had a spare tire. Who doesn't? What could he of done? When your number's up, your number's up. You remember Frank?"

Loretta's face turns ashy white. In half a second her lip is quivering. Good thing I'm up.

"Excuse us, Andy," I say shrilly, jumping to a stand. The blood rushes down from my head and I'm dizzy as hell, but I grab Loretta by the arm and yank her to her feet. "We gotta get some water on us or we'll fry."

Loretta's a zombie, just from the mention of poor Frankie. She doesn't resist, doesn't even remember she has brand new oil on her back that she'll have to do again, doesn't say a single word. "Pull up your straps," I command. She pulls them up. I hold her hand tight and run her down a path between blankets and umbrellas, through a torrent of curses from frisbee players, between cherubs filling sand buckets, and into the cloudy brown froth so fast she's under water before I have to hear her sob.

• • •

Time has always passed, but for years I hardly noticed. I went to work every day on the same subway from the same station and got off at Thirty-fourth Street and walked to just west of Eighth Avenue and went up the elevator to the ninth floor and typed there for Hacker Zippers. Day after day, year after year. First the old man himself, Julius Hacker, and then his son, Marvin, ran the place, both of them roll-up-your-sleeve guys with blood pressure up off the charts and hair lines that receded before my very eyes. I was the girl they could count on to be nice to clients on the phone if *we* were late and bitchy as hell to suppliers if *they* were. The Hackers always gave a very decent bonus at the end of the year. Sometimes the language got rough, but I gave as good as I got, and if a new boy on the floor was fresh I put him in his place. After awhile, more Spanish talkers started working there, no problem to me: I learned a few words of Spanish myself and did some fancy dancing at the Christmas parties.

In my area, near my desk, I've got one window. It's streaked and grimy with city dirt, maybe never been washed in its life (or mine). But I look down at the hat factory on the seventh floor in the building across. For more than twenty years I've let my eyes rest on those stacks of colored felt, the finished goods piled helter-skelter on racks— berets, pill boxes, toques, imitation Stetsons. Especially in winter dusk, when my own office is so dark no matter how many lights are on, I love to look down and see that overlit floor, the dazzle of felts and ribbons against a whole drab city. That's been one of the best parts of my day. Then there's lunch. A long time ago I'd go to Chock Full O'Nuts for the cream cheese and date nut sandwich, or I'd get a hot dog and then head into Macy's. (Now I go to salad bars.) My favorite shopping used to be Korvettes but it's long gone; even Orbachs and Gimbels disappeared. That I learned to live with. It didn't affect what I call my quality of life.

Things never really went downhill until the Velcro. No way could Marvin keep afloat with just the zippers, so he added Velcro. Okay, that wasn't so bad. As he used to joke, he was still at least in openings and closings. But then before I knew it I was working for a Velcro company with maybe half as many workers, no union, no bonus, alcohol-free Christmas parties, and a curly blond-haired boss named Edmond Hall who maybe just got out of college. His first day, he sneered at my typewriter and said, "Next week the computer will be here. Dispose of that thing."

Nothing had ever gone wrong with my Selectric. "I don't know computers," I said.

"You'll learn," he muttered, not even looking at me to my face, but pawing through his stack of phone messages. "What's with this 'Bobbi' business? You're Roberta, right?"

"Everybody calls me Bobbi, so I sign Bobbi."

"Bobbi, Bobbi, Bobbi." He smirked when he said my name and made it sound like it was dirty. "Bobbi, you dot your i's with circles. You know when that went out? With my mother's high school yearbook." He tossed all the little pink message pages on my desk and vanished.

In my head I filed him under "J," for jerk.

• • •

Still sandy from the beach, Loretta and I are out on my terrace drinking a blended yogurt and blueberry thing, craving our old daiquiris. Next door, to my south in this row of identical, two-family brick houses, they all come out onto *their* terrace, too: Esther and her two pale, lumpy daughters who should've flown the coop long ago (but are far too large for lift-off now) and a couple of their girlfriends, similar in looks. It's amazing the deck holds them. Loretta gawks indiscreetly, then rolls her eyes. Esther has just doused the coals of the barbecue grill with lighter fluid, hurling it from the can with the confidence of a practiced arsonist. The gasoline smell wafts over to us instantly. I am always the first stop on the express line of all my neighbors' nauseating odors.

Two more washed-out, bulbous pals emerge on that deck, like it's some kind of reunion. "Oh no," says Loretta, "the footings'll give."

We watch the giggly hullabaloo of hugs and greetings. Gigantic plastic soda bottles get passed and poured as the mounds of flesh arrange themselves around the deck—we listen for the creaking and groaning of stressed timbers—and, settled in place, smile at one another benignly. But it's not like these girls are as harmless as they make out here. Uh-uh. They are inflicted on the whole neighborhood as supermarket cashiers, the ones who never know the cost of unmarked items and shriek a hundred times to some illiterate poor schlub in back to get a price you've spent the last five minutes telling them. Believe me, at work these girls are slow and mean and full of nasty comments. Because of them, you can't get out of Waldbaum's without a stroke.

"Loretta, be careful!" I cry out as she's about to light a cigarette.

"It's only my fourth one today," she says defensively. (Like hell it is. She buried five or six just on the beach.)

"No, not that. I mean the fumes, the flame. You might blow us up."

She gestures over to Esther's own cigarette hanging out between her lips as she hovers over the grill, dropping on meat patties the size of saucers. We can hear the sizzle. Flames jump. Loretta screws up her nose at the first whiff of burning fat. Drifting our way in record time are clouds of dark smoke, carrying suspended globules of cholesterol that will certainly condense over here, like acid rain.

"That's it. I can't take it," says Loretta, rising to her feet. "Bobbi, do you still keep liquor under the sink?"

"Loretta, don't. It's not worth it. You've been so good."

But she disappears into the apartment, quickly returns with my dusty bottle of rum, and pours a shot into her yogurt thing.

"That's disgusting," I say.

"So are they," she retorts, twisting her nose up in the direction of my neighbors. Esther is turning burgers with an oversized spatula, the cigarette wagging in her mouth as she talks. I catch the faintest whisper of sea breeze in the air, a brief briny marine scent floating on a cool current, but it's overpowered and squashed by a hot tornado funnel of leaden beef smoke.

Loretta holds out her glass in a toast. "Hey, Frankie, this one's for you." She sips, grimaces, pours in another long slurp of rum, sips again. I wonder if this means progress that, with a little rum, she can say her old heartthrob's name herself, without breaking down.

The girls next door have a giggling fit, six bowls of human gelatin (unflavored) are a-ripple. Loretta winces, like they're laughing at her. Of course they're not, but Loretta has always worried that everybody's neighbors would know about her and Frank and talk. Even in high school she was secretive about him, as if what they had was something special and not your average backseat fling. And when he got Belinda pregnant and married *her* instead, two weeks after graduation, Loretta swore the truest love would win and she'd be loyal. So for nearly thirty more years she'd been so careful, so discreet, figuring Frank's wife never knew a thing, right 'til the end. (Fat chance.) Once a week they got together, very quiet. Not like Tony Peltz, who leaves his Mister Softee truck running every afternoon when he disappears to call on Barbara Portafino. (Imagine, God help us, getting it on with Mister Softee.) It doesn't matter to Tony if kids are still straggling along with their sweaty dollar bills in hand, or if every tenant from Commodore co-ops is lining up for ice cream in hundred degree heat at his next stop. Nope. And so what if *my* whole block goes bonkers listening to that simple-minded mechanical wind-up tune he lets play over and over and over again, de-dah-de-dah-dah-de-dah-daaah-de-dah, de-daah-de-daah-de-daaah-dah, for more than half an hour nonstop (a quickie for Barbara being endless for us). It's not what you'd call a quiet affair, this Tony Peltz thing.

But Loretta's was different. Classier, she thought.

"Why me?" she asks now, already a little looped. I was afraid this would happen. "Three, maybe four hours a week, that's all I had him. How many total hours are there in a week? Seven times twenty-four.

What is that?"

I'm good at numbers. "A hundred sixty-eight."

"Okay, so what's, like, the percentage of three hours outta one sixty-eight?"

This time I need a few seconds more. "Less than two percent."

For a moment she is silent, her face a blank, while this news sinks in. "Okay," she charges on, "so I had less than two percent of him. Lots less. I never saw him around the big holidays. They'd go on vacation a coupla weeks a year. Sometimes one of the kids' birthdays fell on a fuckin' Tuesday. So for maybe like one and a half percent of his time, maximum, he still had to die when he was with me. Why? Why me?"

"Not just you," I say. "Married men die in other women's beds all the time." Her eyebrows shoot up. I notice, suddenly, how much more they're pencilled in now, how much less real brow than there once was.

"Like Franklin Roosevelt," I continue. "He died in some woman's bed."

"No shit!"

"In Arkansas or somewhere. A spa where he went for his polio."

She nods, smiles, downs a swig of her drink, indifferent to the unmistakable stench of charring flesh now wafting by. "Okay. Franklin Roosevelt. So who else?"

I pause. She's called my bluff. "I can't remember."

She scowls deeply at me. "Roberta. You mean to tell me Roosevelt and Frank Morelli are what you call all the time?"

I shrug. "Not everybody makes the news," I offer in my own defense. "We just don't hear about them all."

"Yeah, right." She finishes off the yogurt-blueberry-rum thing in a long slurp. "Shit. Being a saint was never enough for Belinda Morelli. No. Now she can be fuckin' Eleanor Roosevelt, too."

When Loretta drinks, she gets a mouth and starts to sound a lot like me. So then I don't know what or who to sound like. My choices seem to be like her, all trusting and true-hearted, which is impossible, or even more foul than my own usual, which I'd rather not start up. So I sit quietly for a moment. Next door, clots of ketchup are smeared on blackened meat by pudgy pale paws, and meanwhile Esther, who never sits, slaps another round of burgers on the grill. In seconds, a whole new puff of acrid smoke sails up in our direction, as fresh drippings splatter on the coals.

"Bobbi, y'know what I think?"

"What do you think, Loretta?"

"I think"—she giggles just a bit now—"I think, no more of this older men business. I'm finished with all that. You should be, too."

Something's wrong here. My sugar daddy phase ended long ago, and neither age nor death had much to do with it. And both my actual ex-husbands were a good five years my junior. Loretta herself used to wonder if that meant I was immature. Was that too far back to even count? These facts, however, I don't belabor. Going straight for the jugular is so much faster.

"Hey, Loretta, Frank was six months younger 'n you, remember?"

"No!" she declares adamantly. "He was not!"

"Loretta! You know damn well. He always was. You never let a year go by without discussing it." (Ad nauseam, with me.)

"But he was an old man, Bobbi! He died of a heart attack."

Now I have to really say it. "He was forty-seven, Loretta. The exact same age as us."

She opens her mouth to speak, then closes it. Suddenly, all those little tiny lines around her lips get deeper, like something must be folding inward. She picks up her glass, but it's empty. She holds it anyway, circling it with both her hands.

"I'm sorry," I say.

She laughs a very phony laugh. "Hey. What's to be sorry?"

I can't look at her and she can't look at me, so together we look at the terrace next door just in time to see the contents of a jumbo pack of frankfurters tumble onto the grill.

• • •

They're just three kids, three little girls, really, fifteen or sixteen at the most, swinging around the pole in the middle of the subway car. One's Spanish, one's Chinese, one's black, all giddy and giggly and making lots of noise on the early morning D train crawl through Brooklyn. Their purple-painted fingernails and delicate dark knuckles clutch the metal, letting three skinny bodies float free, then snap taut, float out free again, pull in close, back and forth with the motion of the train. These kids know what they can get away with: skin tight jeans, swaying hips, and bad talk about boys.

"That Jimmy, what a hunk!" says one of the girls, and then, lowering her voice to a deep confidential murmur, she's drowned out by the screech of brakes.

Doors open, people flow in, a few get out, doors close.

"And when he walks!" shrieks the little Spanish girl, puffing out her pelvis in imitation of a strut. They all dissolve in laughter.

Pretty soon the men in this car start to squirm. Nothing is so humbling as smart young girls from the whole entire world talking sexy and like who gives a hoot. Across from me, a lanky suit with wire-rimmed glasses and a *Wall Street Journal* removes his stare from my fingernails (which I've been filing), gets up, walks to the end of the car, and stands by a door, his back arched irritably toward the kids.

"And have you *seen* the way he does it?" asks the Chinese girl, packing a lethal dose of scorn into a single syllable.

Does what? we wonder, we groggy grown-ups fitted shoulder-to-shoulder, thigh-to-thigh, as more people insist on wedging themselves into these crowded seats. The air conditioner whirs but is no match for the humidity, even this early in the day. Two tough MTA repair crew types in sweaty T-shirts clutch their hardhats in one hand, lunch boxes in the other, listening to the kids. Their own conversation's over.

"And that other one in the back row. What's with him? No brains?"

"Uh-uh," says the black girl, face deadpan. "No balls." Silence follows. Then a torrent of knowing cackles bursts from all three.

Well, that's it for this car. Three little girls not only *say* the word balls, they *laugh* at it, and the whole train's done for. Every single woman in the car (even the Orthodox wigged one) bites on her lip to control a smirk. The men stare at the ceiling, touch at their pimples and shaving cuts, push their knees together, spread their knees apart again, glance down at their newspapers, observe the helplessness of their ankles peeking out above their socks, look up again, read the ad for Lavelle School for the Blind in English and Spanish, and get up to wait near the doors long before their real stops, even as we're snail-pacing over the Manhattan Bridge.

For a minute I remember what it's like to be those girls, living smack in the center of life. We were once girls just like them, Loretta and me, before we started drifting to the margins. But maybe we didn't even drift; maybe we didn't move at all. The pit of my stomach goes thud when I think about this. Maybe, instead, life itself moved, expanded, bulged out in different directions, while we clung somehow to the same old spot, once the center, now far to the edge. Like the yolk sticking effortlessly to one side of a frying egg, while the white flows out ahead. A shiver runs up my spine, and the purple polish (only slightly darker than those kids') goes onto my thumbnail in trembling waves, even though we're at a standstill at Grand Street. The rescue job I attempt globs on much too thick.

Loretta notices and shakes her head; she doesn't believe I *still* can't get this right—she who can perfectly outline her lips or brush on mascara or put in contacts when the train's barreling along, lights flickering. Lately, though, since Frank died and she doesn't sleep so great, her whole number's done before I even meet her at the station. Today, her hair, teased out not quite so high and fluffy as usual, is bright orange-red, her lipstick the same. The tone of her pancake makeup is carefully matched, too. But already it's starting to crack along her laugh lines.

"I don't even *want* to be young again," I say, out of the blue. So let her give me another one of her what-the-hell-are-you-talking-about looks.

But she's already there, somehow, right inside the conversation. "I'm not sure anymore. I mean, if I look my age, how will I meet a guy?"

I don't know why, but I get a lump in my throat. Like, *now* she's worried. What about all those years she made do with Frank's crusts and crumbs, his lousy Tuesday evenings (home by ten)? She never talked about meeting guys *then*. Loretta's been my best friend for forty years, but I still don't get her thing with Frank.

"Maturity's good," I say.

"Oh yeah?" She raises one of her penciled brows at me. "Tell me about it."

"No more of those emotional roller-coasters."

She guffaws. "Speak for yourself."

"Really," I insist. "Look at them." By now the three girls are pressing at the door, impatient to get out at 14th Street. Their three sets of eyes dart impishly about as they whisper inside their huddle; then they burst, in unison, into the crooning, moaning stanza of some pop song and move their shoulders sensually in the only dance there's room for in this crowd, their eyes closed, lips open. "They're totally at the mercy of their hormones," I say.

The train lurches to a stop, the doors open, and the girls are gone. Loretta rolls her eyes. "And we're not?"

A dozen new people push inside, the doors close, and the train starts up again.

"It's not the same." I finish the nails on my right hand, smoothly and evenly. One hand, at least, won't need repairs. "Really." I twist the top of the nail polish bottle carefully, as the train speeds up toward Twenty-third Street. "Who was it said youth is wasted on the young? Honestly, Loretta, if you ask me, they can have it."

• • •

It's now exactly one month to the day. When I picked up the phone that night one month ago, Loretta was already sobbing and I thought, first, oh God, it's Tuesday, Frank's night, what if he stood her up? What if he finally decided to can the whole thing?

"I think he's gone," were the first words she stammered out. Just as I'd suspected, the bastard, and believe me there was no satisfaction in having guessed. She went on sobbing for a whole minute, and like an idiot I let her. How could I have known? It took me awhile before I figured out what she was telling me.

"He's in my bed. He doesn't move, he doesn't breathe!" She got those words out okay, then the sobs started all over again.

"Oh no," I mumbled. That was the best I could do. "Oh no. Oh no."

"Bobbi, you gotta help me move him."

"Move him? Loretta, get ahold of yourself. You can't move him! Maybe he's still alive. Did you call 911?"

She answered with sobs.

"Okay, Loretta. I'll call. I'm calling right now. You just..."

"But you *can't* let them find him here! Out in the hall, maybe, but not *here!* Oh help me, Bobbi!"

I took a deep breath. "Loretta, that's the movies. This is real. You gotta leave him where he is. You understand? I'm calling 911 now, and then I'll be right there."

I ran the six blocks and EMS hadn't even come yet. But there was Frank, very gray in the face, cold as ice, buck naked, in Loretta's red, fake satin sheets. The EMS knock on the door came a minute later. And it was over.

Over. Over. But how could twenty-five years be over when you can't even mourn? Poor Loretta. She was too embarrassed to go to the funeral. Lighting candles, saying rosaries, whatever it is you can do by yourself in church, she did all that. But the rituals didn't work. Belinda, the grieving widow, abandoned in the midst of a clear and open life, however passionless (and who's to say?), had her children, her family, her neighbors, her priest. But what did Loretta have, after nearly thirty years spent pining for Tuesday nights? Me. Sitting with her in her kitchen day after day, floundering for some ritual she could hang onto. That's when I thought that maybe we could remember *him* by getting into shape ourselves, a commemoration minus denomination, holy enough. We might still save ourselves from sudden, early death. The running ritual, the food taboos—we started them then, and here we are.

Or are we?

Three days after the slip-up with the rum, I spot Loretta in the checkout line with frozen pepperoni pizzas, a six-pack of Bud, two pounds of liverwurst, a super big bag of potato chips, three cans of Cheeze Whiz, and a gigantic box of chocolate candy. Though I'm not even finished shopping yet, I try to maneuver into the line just behind her, but a very small and very fast old lady shoots between us. So from two carts away, I shout, "Loretta, what are you doing?"

"Leave me alone!" she shouts back.

"Loretta, please, think before you buy all that." She is already emptying things from her cart onto the counter.

"Go away!" she retorts.

The little woman turns to me. "What are you bothering that girl for?"

"We're friends."

"*She* doesn't seem to think so."

"Loretta!" I shout again, over the head of this meddler. "Loretta, wait! Don't do it!"

The old woman clicks her tongue. "Yelling like that. You should be ashamed of yourself. You're old enough to know some manners."

"Lady, it's a long story. I need to talk to her."

"So call her up when you get home!" she orders.

Helplessly, I watch the cashier—an immense girl with dirty-blond hair, one of my neighbors' friends—push through Loretta's ten thousand grams of saturated fat. And Loretta bags for herself, which she never ever does, just to get away from me.

"Loretta, please!"

The cashier is already ringing up the old lady, who glares at me contemptuously while Loretta grabs her bag and stomps out of the store.

The cashier stuffs the woman's cottage cheese and marked-down day-old rolls into a bag and then looks at me. "You have too many items for this lane, ma'am." She folds her pale sausage arms in front of her huge chest. "This is the express lane. Ten items or less."

I glance down at the motionless conveyor belt and count. "It's only twelve."

"A rule is a rule."

"C'mon, I just wanted to talk to my friend in this line."

She rolls her eyes. "That's *my* problem?"

"So call her at home," says the old woman as she finishes adjusting her grocery bag into a larger canvas tote. "Whatsa matter, you don't have a telephone?"

"Ten items or less," says the cashier.

I remove a quart of skim milk and a box of oat bran and stick them in the magazine rack. "There. It's ten."

The clerk shakes her head. "Uh-uh. You'll have to put them back on the shelves where they belong or get into another line, ma'am. If I let you through, I'd have to let *everybody* through."

A bony knuckle raps me on the shoulder. "Don't make trouble," says the old man behind me with a Russian accent as thick as the humid evening air. "You're holding things up. I have medication to take." Behind him is another angry face. I change lines.

Back on the street, it feels like a thunderstorm should happen; the purple sky is cracked with a streak of eerie yellow light and there's nothing to breathe. On my block, the deserted Mr. Softee truck churns out the old moronic tune while kids sit and fidget on the curb. It's a miracle none of them have taken a sledge hammer to that vehicle yet. De-dah-de-dah-dah-de-dah-daaah-de-dah, de-dah-de-dah-de-daaah-dah.

When I get to my building, Loretta's sitting on the stoop, her bag of groceries beside her, her tight skirt hitched to the top of her skinny thighs and the stiletto heels arranged neatly beside her stockinged feet. My mother used to call her a floozy because of the way she dressed; my mother was *so* naïve. As I get closer, I see that her cheeks are wet and streaked black with runny eye-liner, which she hasn't bothered to wipe away. She smiles anyway.

"Hi, Bobbi," she says timidly.

I hesitate on the step beside her and linger for a bit. The song of the Mister Softee truck drones on and on, on and on and on and on.

"Hey, Loretta," I say. "How about a daiquiri?"

She hoists herself up and follows me into the house.

The Menorah Girl

I.

It was the shortest day of the year, and it was Brooklyn. Though the windows rattled with every gust of wind and the whole building hummed when the trains came in at Ditmas Avenue, we could still hear the drone of prayers from the synagogue down the street. A light sleet had just begun to fall and the rapid onset of dusk cast a hush over the line of traffic stopped at the light below. From our lookout on the third floor we saw a slow-moving stream of stooped men in black coats and black hats and black beards fade into the grayness of Fourteenth Avenue. Across the street the lights went out in the dry cleaner's and the shoe repair. We watched the candy store owner pull the metal grates over the doorway as he closed up. Minute by minute, everything outside grew a little grayer, a little colder.

In Aunt Shirley's bedroom the radiator hissed. My cousin Marty and I sat in the dark on the edge of the big bed, mesmerized by the glow of headlights that burst and scattered into a million colors on the drops, half rain now, half sleet, that slid down the window panes. Marty took my hand and held it tightly.

"Blip minkaburnie rotag," he said.

"Arikna voomtrig galutner," I answered. "Nepresal?"

"Zip zie."

Our secret language had no vocabulary or translation, only sounds that emerged from the deepest places in our hearts where we had the perfect understanding of two ten-year-olds in love. Marty lived here in Brooklyn and I lived far upstate, but at Christmas vacation my mother brought me from our little farm to this city, which had already become, to me, the essence of all life and love, for even as a child I felt starved for the world's dazzle and excitement. Climbing trees, planting radishes, breathing all that clean fresh country air, I feared that the important things in life were already passing me by and were, in fact, forbidden.

And so at about the age of ten I began to do so many things in secret, knowing somehow that my sense of deprivation would not be taken seriously if I voiced it. In secret I wrote the magazine columnists and asked them to rescue me from a slow and tortuous death by boredom, but no matter how minutely I described the tedium of garden-weeding and the desolation of having no friends within five miles, they never wrote back. Nor did the hosts of television game shows whom I wrote covertly, begging them to send me one of those encyclopedias they gave away so freely to folks I knew would never open them, who didn't even *win* the games but got World Books and Britannicas as consolation prizes. "Surely you could spare just one," I wrote. "I'm stuck out here. The library's too far to walk and I need information. Even L to P would help," I said, thinking that if the whole set were just too bulky, the volumes containing London, Moscow, New York, and Paris would suffice. But not even a form letter came my way.

In secret, too, I nursed my craving for religion. There was no synagogue and God was mentioned so little in our house I thought perhaps He was not Jewish, though by then I knew that Eddie Cantor and Mort Sahl were, Rosemary Clooney and Perry Como were not. Most Italians were not. Most blondes were not. To teach these things, I surmised, was my mother's intent in scrimping for our first TV. "Cantor!" she would exclaim during the Ed Sullivan show, cracking walnuts in her bare hands. "He must have changed it from Kantowitz." "She pretends she's not," I learned of several actresses, "but she is." And that was the extent of my religious education. When no one else was in the house I stole the Bible from the bookcase much as other children must have stolen *Peyton Place*.

Being in love with my own cousin was yet another secret, but during our winter reunions, at least, Marty and I were partners in taboo. We would sneak out of our grandmother's house, where first we'd meet, and roam the streets to Chester Avenue, only two blocks away but a world given over entirely to another forbidden delight: Christmas. Every house on Chester Avenue had strings of colored lights in the windows and immense nativity scenes in the front yards. We knew we were not supposed to believe in what they meant, but we coveted them and the great swollen Santa Claus faces that bulged from the front doors and the reindeer with blinking lights for eyes.

"Schuf won biknik," said Marty longingly.

"Arnival plantril," I replied, squeezing his hand.

Fate had sealed us away from Christmas, just as it had sealed us away from each other, for we had known for years already that as cousins we could never marry. But on Chester Avenue, as if in some foreign country, we held hands anyway. We could be in love and we could have Christmas before turning back onto Clara Street to Bubbie's.

This night, a few blocks away at Aunt Shirley's, we looked out not on Christmas lights but from one empty window onto an entire neighborhood of empty windows. Just one building was different: across the street, two flights up from the candy store, was the apartment from which a cheerful electric menorah would signal to us after dark from the window of every room. We sat and waited.

Suddenly the bedroom door burst open and the light went on. We jumped.

"What? You're in *here?*" exclaimed Aunt Hannah, Marty's mother, as she clutched her chest. "What are you doing sitting in the dark?" she asked accusingly. But then she saw how frightened we were, and her own expression softened. She was a beautiful woman with eyes often filled with anger and thick chestnut hair hidden in a bun. She judged sternly and quickly, and sometimes she forgave with a touch of majesty, and so we felt both relieved and blessed when she laughed.

"Shirley, Muriel, come see this," she called to her sisters in the next room. Then she switched the light back off.

"What are you doing sitting in the dark? You'll go blind!" shouted Shirley, her hand on her chin in a gesture of perpetual worry.

"Crazy kids," was all my mother said. She was the youngest of seven sisters. She may have grown plump and taken to wearing ugly farm oxfords, Hannah's blouses may have been cut the lowest, revealing the fullest breasts, and skinny Shirley may more often have placed her hands on her hips in the most angular and scornful pose, but they were all of a piece, these sisters: fair-skinned, sharp-tongued, and smart, and on the phone it was difficult even for us, their children, to tell their voices apart.

Shirley turned on the light. "In the dark they must be up to no good."

"Oh, leave them alone," scolded Hannah, turning the switch off again. "They're only playing a game."

My mother asked, "Ellen, what are you doing in here?"

I said, "We're playing a game."

Marty said, "We're up to no good."

Aunt Hannah turned the light off and the three of them went back into the kitchen. Their bursts of laughter and murmurs of confidence reached us in little puffs, like the smells of soup boiling and veal roasting, as we waited for the lights to go on in the menorah rooms. Up and down the street other lights went on, one by one. Down below we saw Uncle Harvey trudge along the sidewalk, returning from his job at the post office and carrying little bags of groceries. He kicked slush from his galoshes as he turned toward the doorway. We saw the dentist from the second floor apartment leave, pulling his collar snugly around his ears. We saw old Mrs. Levertov from the first floor push her grocery cart along, against the light, oblivious to the traffic and honking.

"Thatta way, Mrs. L," chuckled Marty.

No lights shone yet in the menorah rooms, so I crept out to the living room to watch my uncle's arrival.

"You're late!" Shirley announced as she picked bags of food from him like fruit from a tree. He stood motionless until she had picked him clean. Then, slowly and methodically, he unwound from his scarf, overcoat, and gloves. He was a solid, sluggish man who always sounded as if he had food in his mouth.

"You shouldn't know what's going on in that post office," he said as he put his hat on the foyer table.

"Not *there*, Harvey!" snapped Shirley. "It's dripping wet!"

"They've got sixteen extra men on and it's a crazy house. You'd think if the packages didn't get delivered by Christmas the world would collapse. It's *meshugah*, I tell you."

Shirley said, "Where are the mushrooms?"

"What mushrooms?"

"They were on the *list*, Harvey!"

He shrugged. "They were? I didn't see. Honest, I didn't see. So we'll go without mushrooms. Big deal."

Shirley laughed. "Veal and mushrooms for dinner, I've been planning for a week, and we'll go without mushrooms, he says. Easy for him to say!" She went back into the kitchen. "So we'll go without mushrooms," she mimicked.

"So I ask you," said Harvey, lumbering behind her. "Would the United States Post Office put sixteen extra men on for Rosh Hashanah?"

We had been summoned to the table before the lights came on in the menorah windows and sat fidgeting. Another uncle had arrived.

"Jack, will you quit it please!" snapped Hannah, jerking her shoulder away from her husband.

Uncle Jack wiped fog from his glasses. "All I want is one lousy kiss, and what a battle I get."

"You'd think he hadn't touched a woman in years," Hannah said.

"Sometimes it seems that way," he retorted.

"Not in front of the children," warned my mother, spooning out noodle pudding. "Sit down, Jack, you're just in time."

Jack patted Marty and me on the head. "Martha and Walter aren't here yet, I see."

"The *store*, Jack," said Hannah. "The week before Christmas you don't leave a clothing store just because there's dinner."

"So what do we do for dessert?" he asked, winking at me. "What'll we do if Martha doesn't bring us chocolate cake?"

Shirley laughed. "We'll have Mrs. Levertov's brownies."

Harvey had just bitten into a slice of rye bread. "That woman never stops baking," he said, garbling his words.

"Swallow before you talk," said Shirley.

Harvey swallowed. "That woman never stops baking."

"We heard you the first time," said Shirley.

For a few moments there was only the sound of cutlery on china as everyone concentrated on eating. Suddenly Marty stood up, dashed into the bedroom, and ran back out again. I watched carefully for his signal. He shook his head "no."

"Sit still and eat or you won't get a brownie," said Shirley, smirking. "She's always baking, that crazy lady. The smells come up through the vent in the bathroom and could knock you right out. You can smell chocolate at five in the morning. You can smell bread baking at eleven at night."

Harvey said, "She lives all by herself. Who eats it?"

Hannah smirked. "Maybe she supports an orphanage somewhere."

"Or an underdeveloped nation," Shirley rolled her eyes.

"God help them," laughed Hannah. "You could choke to death on her brownies, right? Dry like the desert last time."

"Come on," chided my mother, the voice of fairness. "She means well. She knew the Rosenbergs, you know."

Shirley rolled her eyes again. "Who *doesn't*? Every year she goes out and marches in the demonstration. She's seventy-five years old and swears she'll live until the Rosenbergs are vindicated."

"Lotsa luck," said Harvey. "She'll be here forever."

"Who are the Rosenbergs?" I asked.

"She couldn't be seventy-five," said my mother. "Mama's seventy-five. Look at the difference."

"Only her hairdresser knows for sure," quipped Marty.

"Who are the Rosenbergs?" I asked again.

"They live across the street," replied Shirley.

"She gets face lifts. Must have had her third by now," said Hannah.

"I don't think that's so." Harvey tried to be kind. "She's a poor woman. She doesn't have a cent."

"Except for our rent, of course," snapped Shirley.

"Yours!" cried Hannah. "If she had *ours*, she would have had her neck and tushie lifted too by now!"

"Mama looks like she could be Mrs. Levertov's mother," said my mother.

"Poor Mama, as if she didn't have enough trouble being *our* mother!"

"Imagine *anyone* being Mrs. Levertov's mother!"

The three sisters laughed. Then Shirley brought an aluminum foil package from the kitchen. We watched as she unpeeled the crumpled ends, revealing the block of brownies. With a great flourish she took a carving knife and finished the cuts that had been made partway between the dark brown squares. Even from where I sat I could see the brownies shatter. My mouth watered.

"Here, boobalah, have a brownie," Shirley said, amassing a million crumbs on a plate and sliding it to me. And although the others laughed, I savored the first crumbs. To me the dry morsels were a delicacy, as exotic and exciting as the Christmas lights on Chester Avenue.

Marty had sneaked away from the table; now he emerged from the bedroom. "They're on!" he announced, grinning broadly. I pushed away my plate and raced to join him.

Our waiting was a solemn ritual. We stared at the three menorahs in the three windows across the street and were soon rewarded. In unison we cried out, "There she is!"

And there she was, in the most brightly lit room, the farthest menorah to the left, a girl who walked across the room, as she had the night before and on three occasions the previous year, without a stitch of clothing, a girl naked and unashamed right across the street. Only for a second did we catch a glimpse of her entire body. Then we pieced her together from the parts we saw to one side of the curtain or above the window sill, filling in with our imaginations what was still behind a table or hidden by a chair. For a few seconds she stood at her dresser and we could see the silhouette of her young, firm breasts. Then she turned and we could see her buttocks. She turned again and for a fleeting moment we could see the mysterious dark triangle. We watched, dumbstruck and intent. A kimono swirled around in a scarlet circle, obstructing the view. Then the light went off. The menorah twinkled, alone against the dark. We saw a new motion, a red kimono entrance into the next room, where a shade was pulled halfway down the window, meeting the topmost flame of another electric menorah. That was all. We waited a few minutes but nothing more happened. The spectacle of the menorah girl, for that night, had come to an end.

II.

A DOZEN YEARS LATER OR SO, WHILE I was working as a teacher in Paris, Marty came to visit during his summer vacation. I met him at the passport checkpoint at Orly Airport. It was nine o'clock in the morning Paris time, three o'clock his. He was bleary-eyed and haggard from the trip, but I thought the gaunt look was fitting for a man who had just finished up a long and difficult romance. We had not seen each other for awhile, but he was the same old Marty: clean shaven and conservatively dressed in a sports coat and khaki trousers, easy to find in an airport teeming with American kids in torn blue jeans and long hair. But he still had his wild-eyed musician look and all the familiar gestures: he blew his nose a lot, nervously stomped out half-smoked cigarettes one after another, and furrowed his brow deeply.

At his request I had found a small hotel on the Right Bank, where he would be near the museums and the opera, and I left him there to take his nap and antihistamines. Later he crossed over to the Left Bank and met me at André's in the thirteenth *arrondissement*.

My friend André, the good doctor, suave host, enchanting lover, master of small talk, insisted on taking us out in his little gold Renault and flaunting his city, which glittered and shone for us as if at his command. We crossed the bridge to the Ile de la Cité and were dazzled by the spread of André's cathedral, then we sped down his Champs Elyseés and around his Arc de Triomphe and along his magnificent boulevards, then up and down the narrow, twisting streets of his Montmartre. Finally he brought us to the twentieth *arrondissement*, where he claimed to feel at home among his people, the immigrant workers. He led us into a narrow, cramped Moroccan restaurant. All the waiters and diners seemed to know him and saluted him with fondness.

"And how are the twin boys?" he asked the proprietor, warmly pumping his hand. "Ah, Said, don't forget, I'll buy that carpet from you!" he called out to a customer. "Pick it up next Tuesday, *d'accord?*" And to a woman working in the back room he said discreetly, "Bring the baby in tomorrow, okay? And I'll have the medication."

He could eat the red-hot harissa sauce by the tablespoon, as if deriving from it his own intense warmth. By then I had learned to sprinkle a few drops on my couscous which, in this restaurant, was the fluffiest and whitest I had ever seen. Marty eyed it suspiciously. André ordered dish after succulent dish, a whole chicken marinated bright turmeric yellow, chunks of lamb in earthen *terrines*, chickpeas with exotic herbs, delicate pastries flavored with rosewater, but Marty could barely touch his food.

"My cousin is not feeling well," I said.

"Of course, the long trip and not enough sleep!" André consoled in a strangely jocular tone, as if he could not really comprehend a failing of appetite caused by such small circumstances. But he leaned forward with true concern etched in his deeply bronzed forehead and asked, "But you'll be all right, *mon vieux*, no? Please, it is important that you let me know."

Strolling back to the car at midnight, Marty was silent and pale while André, growing darker and more intense as the night went on, flirted unabashedly with girls we passed on the Boulevard de Belleville. And what was I doing there? I wondered, no longer useful, it seemed, as cousin or lover. By the time we reached André's apartment, I was overcome by sadness and Marty by an attack of stomach cramps. André drove him to the hotel.

The next day I was filtering coffee for breakfast when André came in, already dressed. "Don't make any for me. I'm going straight to the hospital." I nodded. He said, "I have something for your cousin's stomach. His French is very good, by the way. You must tell him I said so." Oh, the charmer, I thought! "And remind him to take two spoonfuls of this before each meal." He slid a large jar across the counter.

Then he said, "I have a friend coming over tonight and you have to move back into the guest room."

Automatically, I nodded again, but my heart sank. He smiled compassionately. André liked to remain friends with old lovers like me; he took pride in that. When I needed a place to live for two weeks before my new rental was ready, he invited me to stay with him. Our affair had ended once already, over a month before, so there was not supposed to be anything painful in this. But I was down to 110 pounds, an even 50 kilos on the doctor's own scales, a weight I had not been since early in my adolescence. Alas, I was still young and if I could be swept off my feet by him once, why not twice? It was romance, after all, and silent suffering seemed still to be in vogue, and I liked the new way my old clothes fit now.

"What kind of spoonfuls?" I asked.

"There's a measuring spoon in the jar," he said, straightening his tie. His perfectly pressed shirt gleamed white. I could have killed him for looking so good.

"Okay, *d'accord*," I said, knowing I might burst into tears and wishing he would hurry and leave. I hated him.

He leaned forward and smoothed my hair. "You understand, don't you, Ellen?" he asked with that "I can't help it" look in his eye.

"Of course," I said, because what was the use of making another scene? But to myself I thought, drop dead, you bastard.

When Marty came by I was alone in the flat, restraining myself from tearing it apart. I gave him the jar. Inside were little green granules, like nothing we had ever seen before except certain kinds of bubble bath, along with a small white plastic shovel.

"He said take two just before meals," I explained.

Marty insisted he was feeling better. I told him what had happened. "Let's get out of here," he said, crushing a Gauloise *filtre*, and I suggested we go shop for shoes. The sole of one of mine, worn thin, had split in two and now flapped open whenever I took a step. But my feet were very narrow and all the European shoes in my price range seemed to be cut wide, so we wandered around the Left Bank on a mission for cheap, narrow shoes. Near the Mouffetard market I found a pair that fit. They were good for walking and looked reasonably smart, so I took them. I wore them right out of the store and dumped the old pair into the nearest trash can. Good riddance, at least, to old shoes! I thought, feeling slightly cheered.

But by the time we reached the Place du Panthéon, which was not so very far, it became clear that the new shoes were much too small.

"They'll stretch," Marty reassured, but optimism from him was hardly comforting. He led me into a café on the rue Sufflot where we sat at a small table in the sun. Marty opened the jar and shoveled two teaspoons of bubble bath granules into his mouth. We each had a glass of wine and a *croque monsieur* for lunch. But right afterwards Marty excused himself and ran to the bathroom, where he stayed for half an hour. Waiting, I massaged my feet; I already had a blister above my left heel.

III.

I LAY ON MY GRANDMOTHER'S BED listening to Christmas carols on the radio. The music seemed so beautiful to me. I had closed the door because I knew the others would not want to hear and I feared it might be wrong to even listen. A large portrait of my grandmother's father stared down from the wall. He wore a black cap and his hair and beard were a blondish red, and although there was the same kindly twinkle in his bright blue eyes as in my mother's, aunts', and grandmother's, I thought of him as being very old and stern. What would he think of Christmas carols?

"Hark the herald angels sing, glory to the newborn king. Peace on Earth, and mercy mild, God and sinners reconciled..." I hummed along with the tune.

"Not until *Friday*, and that's final!" My mother's shout came from the kitchen. She was on the phone, talking to my father home upstate. I tensed, afraid of what I would hear next. A low murmur, words indistinguishable. "God rest ye merry gentlemen, let nothing you dismay, remember Christ our sa-a-vior was born..." Not my savior, I knew, but I did not know why. I looked up at my great grandfather on the wall: his eyebrows seemed to knit closer. Perhaps he was worrying about my mother; perhaps he was worrying about me. Was *he* my savior? What *was* a savior?

"I don't care, Howie!" I heard her say, finishing with an awful sob. I rolled over and turned the radio up so it would blot out her voice and her sobs. Then I went to the window, which looked out on Clara Street. Directly across was Aunt Martha's house. From her rear windows could be seen the back of Aunt Bella's building, which we entered on Tehama Street. Then, across Tehama was where Aunt Ida lived. Shirley and Hannah lived about twelve blocks away. The sisters had all stuck together except for my mother, who had married a farmer and moved so far away I sensed the others felt sorry for her.

"Damn him!" my mother's voice penetrated my Christmas music. Then grating, rumbling noises like furniture being moved brusquely about came from the direction of the kitchen. A stir. A commotion. My mother. My stomach did a somersault.

"Muriel, stop!" I heard my grandmother call.

And then came the sound of those horrible sobs. I could not bear to hear my mother cry, not ever, not at home or here or anywhere; it broke my heart and wrenched me right in two. But out came those deep gulping noises and the heavy sniffles, the bellowing gush. No, no, no, I wished with all my might, she has to stop. But she didn't stop, and so I threw myself back on the bed, took my grandmother's feather pillow from under the bedspread, and wrapped it around my ears. And then I could only hear the inside of my head, a steady and low *shwee-shwee-shwee* whispering roar, like a record when it comes to the end, and when I closed my eyes tight I saw light in lines the way the slats in the Venetian blinds on Bubbie's windows made them, only they faded against the inside of my eyelids and were gone. The *shwee-shwee-shwee* roar got louder and faster and made me dizzy so

I forced myself to hear the Christmas carols and sang them to myself. "Away in the manger no crib for a bed, the little lord Jesus lay down his sweet head, the stars in the sky looked down..." I tried to imagine sleeping in the hay. Hay is for horses; that's what the kids at school said when you said, "Hey, hey there." The cozy little manger. I opened my eyes and stared at the portrait. If I squinted one eye shut it seemed like he was just starting to smile but if I opened that eye and closed the other one I was sure he was about to frown. I changed from one eye to the other, from smile to frown, no crib for a bed the little lord Jesus lay down his sweet head, frown then smile. I took the pillow from around my ears. A man's voice on the radio was reading the news. I turned the radio off. A gust of my Aunt Goldie's laughter blew in under the closed door like a strong, warm breeze, then a murmur of female voices. I waited, holding my breath, preparing for the sobs, for the end of the world. But there was only the murmur. My mother wasn't crying. Next I heard a peal of her laughter. I put on my shoes and ran out.

The kitchen light was very bright. I scrambled onto a chair and a glass of milk appeared in front of me and then, with a "Here, boobahlah" from Goldie, a plate of home-baked marble *mandelbrot* and yeast cakes with swirls of white icing, and with another "Here" from Shirley a package wrapped in foil with blueberry muffins and brownies I recognized as Mrs. Levertov's. I gnawed first at the *mandelbrot* and gulped the milk.

My mother shrugged. "In a million years could I ever figure out what he really wants?" She was talking about my father but didn't seem upset.

Goldie flicked ashes into a saucer. She was the oldest of the sisters, the tallest and the heaviest and the loudest. "He wants maybe you should stay home and make him miserable all day long?"

The sisters all burst out laughing.

"You joke," said Bubbie, coming closer from the recess of the kitchen where she had been working. I observed the solid squareness of her legs, bound in dark pinkish-tan stockings. Her whole short form was rectangular, draped in a square blue cotton dress. "But a marriage is a marriage," she warned. "Remember that."

I stole a quick glance around the table. All four mocking sets of eyes took a roll upward. "Like yours was, huh, Mama?" said Goldie.

"He should just rest in peace," said Bubbie.

Hannah said something in Yiddish and they all laughed, even Bubbie, who blushed deeply. I did not know what Hannah said; Yiddish was *their* secret language. I rummaged in the foil for a brownie. My glass of milk had been mysteriously refilled and I drank it in fast gulps.

While Shirley cleared the table, Bubbie took the silver menorah from a shelf and put it on a kitchen counter. My mother sat across from me and seemed to look straight at me, but I could tell that she didn't even know I was there. She pushed bread and cookie crumbs into a pile on the tablecloth, then traced with one finger the brown rings left by coffee cups. I jumped down from my chair and crept to the stove. Bubbie did not notice as I followed all her movements. I peered with her into a big steel pot. Inside were gray-green rolls of stuffed cabbage; sweet-smelling steam billowed out. She covered the pot, then looked at a chicken in the oven, its skin roasted crisp and gold. She closed the oven door and went back to the menorah. None of her daughters paid attention as she put six candles in, but I watched her square jaws work away in whispers of prayer in a language I never understood, from a world I never knew, but which I sensed, because of the stern devotion on her face, still had the power to protect us.

IV.

IN ONE MORE HOUR I HAD BLISTERS on both feet. Visiting the sights was out of the question, but I dreaded going back to André's, so Marty and I went from café to café down the Boulevard St. Michel. It was a warm and sunny day, lovely for sitting still. Fearful for his stomach, Marty first ordered mineral water and lemon slices, but sobriety in our state was not a good idea. By the third café he grew braver and more desperate and had wine along with me. When queasiness threatened, he shoveled in the green granules. And so from one café to the next we got tipsier and tipsier, until we were absolutely drunk.

Wine loosened up our heartaches and anger and made them easier to exchange; my laments about André and Marty's stories of Corinne, his ex-girlfriend, came pouring out.

"All those nervous breakdowns she nearly had," he ranted. "Do you have any idea how many times I went through those with her? Tearing out to get prescriptions filled in the middle of the night. The nonstop headaches. Menstrual periods that went on for weeks."

"Sounds like a lot of fun."

He rolled his eyes. "Never a dull moment. She'd call up and beg me to come over, then she'd start crying and storming and throw me out, like I was the one who'd started it."

"I can't see why it took you so long to leave her," I teased.

"I didn't leave her," he said, finishing off his glass of wine. He unscrewed the cap to his jar. "She found someone else."

"I know," I said, thinking he could spare himself this part.

"Her shrink advised it." He began to laugh. I watched him scoop up the little green granules and swallow. "A nut case," he said after gulping a water chaser. "A real nut case. How did I get mixed up with a nut?"

"It's no better when they're not nuts," I mused. "Look at my André."

"Yeah," said Marty, "what a smoothie. Fast talker, good looker, slick as hell." He paused and blew smoke rings. "I'm surprised you'd fall for that type."

"Hey, I tried a weird ugly one first, give me credit. But he didn't work out." I sighed. "I wanted romance. I wanted love."

"Who doesn't? You think I was *looking* for the psycho ward?"

He poured out the last of the wine, dividing it carefully between our two glasses. I noticed for the first time an area of his scalp where he was beginning to go bald.

"But boy, was it exciting, Marty. Dinner in those quaint little brasseries. Long crazy drives to the seaside on Sundays. Rendezvous between house calls. And all those compliments in French! *'Que tu es belle!' 'Que tu es sage!'* 'How lovely your eyes, the color of emeralds.' I ate it up."

"You wanted a French lover," said Marty, shaking his head. "You watched too many movies."

I shrugged. "That was part of the magic of being here. In the daytime I was a prim English teacher, giving my boring little lessons. At night I ran off to meet the most handsome man in Paris."

Marty stubbed out a cigarette. Within half a minute he lit another. He looked at me as if trying to remember who I was.

I said, "I knew it wouldn't last, but what the hell? What's so great about the ones that last?"

Marty laughed. "You mean the ones that go, 'leave me *alone*, Jack!'" He mimicked his own mother.

"Shut *up*, Harvey!"

"Goldie, not *knaidlach* again!"

We laughed guiltily. "Is that the only kind of love that lasts?" I asked, but Marty only rolled his eyes in reply.

"I'd never known anyone like him before," I went on drunkenly. "He used to help get Jewish refugees from Morocco into Israel when he was younger. There's a Moroccan tailor upstairs from him. He adores André. He made him a leather suit and gave it to him, free. *Leather!*"

"A charmer, the man's just another charmer!" Marty shouted.

"He's a doctor, for Chrissakes," I shouted back, as if that would explain it all. "And he serves the working class. His office is in a slum. He treats immigrants for free."

"Doctor, heal thyself!" pronounced my drunken cousin as we rose to leave.

Out on the sidewalk my shoes bit in a little deeper and I winced. We headed toward a restaurant on rue Monsieur-le-Prince, Marty swaggering, me limping, while I persisted in the defense of my indefensible friend.

"I was flattered. His patients told him their problems and he told me his."

"This Casanova has problems?"

"He wants to kill his wife."

"Ah-hah!" said Marty. "You might call that a problem." He blew his nose. Then he turned to me, puzzled. "What wife?"

"Ex-wife. Remember, he's older. He's had a whole life already."

Marty began to sing. "He's had a life, and he's had a wife…"

"Sssh," I admonished as we entered the restaurant, already quite crowded. We were shown to a tiny table sandwiched closely between other tiny tables. I tried not to think about the blister, which had just ruptured. "She came last summer and kidnapped their son when André had him rightfully on vacation. She took him back to Sweden. She's Swedish."

"Of course," teased Marty. "What else?"

"Now he wants to kill her. He wakes up in the middle of the night muttering about it."

"How sweet." He lit a cigarette. "How utterly romantic."

I laughed. "You'll read about it in the paper someday."

"*Very* exciting," he said sardonically, and suddenly I felt overwhelmed by the sheer stupidity of it all. How did I ever get involved in such a tangle?

We each ordered the cheapest dinner, *biftek* and *frites* preceded by a thin slice of pâté and pickles. Marty ordered a large carafe of the house wine. A group of five very tall, thin students dressed in the most chic of bohemian styles squeezed around the table to our right, which could not have been designed for more than two. Fitting themselves in, they laughed and carried on, but they all fell into a hush and stared when Marty drew a full shovelful of bath crystals from his jar and emptied them into his mouth. I noticed his tongue had become green. The wine was delivered just as he swallowed, and he washed the crystals down with it. The students then resumed their banter.

"I just wanted it to be simple," I said.

"All you wanted was true love, huh?"

"He was terrific," I sighed, forgetting the morning's conversation.

"He was a sadist and a would-be murderer," countered Marty.

"He was romantic," I insisted.

Marty held his wine glass up in a toast. "To romance!" he proposed. We clinked glasses. The students next to us were suddenly quiet again.

"To sadism, murder, and romance!" I said, touching glasses again.

"In other words, to love!" pronounced Marty, clinking glasses one final time. I saw those five finely chiseled Gallic faces smirk at us and didn't care. What could they understand, after all? In this state of tipsiness we spoke English as if it were an impenetrable nonsense language of our childhood. I watched the students: two women, three men, all just a little younger than us, yet perfectly at peace with themselves. The couples hugged and pawed each other with ease and no self-consciousness. I wanted to lean over and ask them how they managed. I looked to Marty to see if he would want to try a few questions on them. But Marty was turning gray, then green, then white, a whole sick kaleidoscope right before my eyes.

"Oh God," he groaned, standing. Then he pushed away his chair and staggered to the men's room.

V.

IN AUNT GOLDIE'S BOOKCASE Marty and I found a play, a silly comedy of manners called *Nevertheless*. The word, which appeared in nearly every scene, enchanted us. Never-the-less. We took it apart and put it back together again. With each utterance it swelled in size and significance. Ne-ver-the-less. We repeated it until its syllables became mere sounds, emanations of our own giddiness. Then we repeated it more until sense returned and magnified, and "nevertheless" superceded in meaning and power all the words we'd ever known and even those we had invented. We cleared ourselves a stage at one end of the room and acted out the play, each of us shifting from role to role.

"Rosamund, I will be yours forever," swore Marty, throwing himself on his knees.

"But I'm Alexandra!" I protested.

"Not *now*!" he cried impatiently. "Turn the page!"

"Oh." I changed my stance. "But, Ernest," I read, "you're engaged to Alexandra and I am marrying Bartholomew in a fortnight!" I did not know what a fortnight was, but pictured it to be some enchanted locale, like a horse-drawn carriage or a gazebo, perhaps, though I did not know what that was, either.

"Nevertheless," pronounced Marty's Ernest, lingering over the pause so we could relish the excitement of the word. He shifted his weight from one pudgy knee to the other and cleared his throat. "Never-the-less," he repeated solemnly, though the repetition was not in the script, "my heart belongs to you and to you alone."

We acted out the play three entire times, and on each occasion that the word arose, we were careful to clear a path of quiet respect through our giggles and to pronounce it with the deference it deserved.

Later at the dinner table Uncle Al wiped a drop of mushroom-barley soup from his little gray moustache and announced that the rye bread was stale.

"I should maybe run out in a taxi now to get fresher?" asked Goldie, carrying more plates in from the kitchen.

"Am I saying you did something wrong?" asked Al, pushing away his empty bowl. Immediately Goldie grabbed it and removed it from the table. "I just said it's stale, that's all. I just made an observation."

Marty said, "Nevertheless, it tastes good."

"Thank you," said Goldie.

Al broke a hard poppy seed roll and waved a piece under Marty's nose. "But this is better," he insisted.

Goldie shrugged her big shoulders. "I got the rye this morning on Thirteenth Avenue. I couldn't have got it fresher if I baked it myself." She crammed a piece of it into her mouth as she took Al's plate to the sink.

Uncle Al shook his head sadly.

My mother said, "Sit down, Goldie. Eat something with us."

I watched Bubbie as she undid the interior of her roll, gently pulling out diaphanous white shreds so that the crusty brown shell was left intact. She heaped the shreds between her soup bowl and mine. Both her elbows were planted squarely on the table as she methodically dipped in her spoon, brought it steaming to her mouth, and slurped it in a steady, deliberate rhythm. I was waiting for my soup to cool, but Bubbie only ate hers boiling hot.

"Eat, *shana kind*," she said to me.

"I will," I said. Marty caught my eye; there was mischief in his smile, and a dare. I watched Bubbie's face as she worked over a morsel of crust with a distant look, as if she were remembering very distinctly a crustier roll in the old country and an even hotter bowl of soup.

"Nevertheless," I said to her, keeping a straight face. "Nevertheless, first I'll wait 'til it cools."

Laughter snorted out through Marty's nose. "The soup will get cold nevertheless," he said.

The grown-ups all scowled at us.

Marty said, "Nevertheless, I'll eat mine hot."

Then the two of us burst into manic giggles, and our mothers soon began to talk about the weather.

It was doomsday eve: the next morning I would go back upstate, Marty back to school. We stood watch for the last time. Our silence was morose and heavy as we clutched hands, sitting on the edge of Aunt Shirley's bed. Down below, the cars drove by in a steady stream. The night was clear and cold; the men in black paraded by with an especially brisk pace, their breath condensing and freezing into hoary white lace upon their beards. The lights in the dry cleaner's went off. Mrs. Levertov came out of the candy store and dashed nimbly between the moving cars. Across the street the kitchen light went on, then the living room lit up, and, finally, the bedroom that was for us so crucial was filled with a soft, rosy-yellow radiance. All the electric menorahs twinkled and it was as if the air itself were electrified, and we ourselves switched on suddenly to the most intense eagerness. Our eyes focused squarely on the bedroom. Our lungs ceased to take in air. And as if on cue, she appeared: a certain fluid style of movement that we knew was hers, a quickness across the room, a flutter of white things, and there she was in all her naked glory.

"There she is!" we sang together.

Breasts, buttocks, thighs, the narrow waist, the angular shoulders, the triangle: for a few final seconds the menorah girl and all her mystery were ours again.

VI.

THE WIZENED HOTEL CONCIERGE seemed to be dozing, and we tried to steal past him. But he opened his eye and said, *"Bon soir,"* as if he had first seen us with his eyes closed and already grown accustomed to the sight. He smiled knowingly as he looked from Marty to me and back to Marty again. I thought I saw him wink. Marty became confused. *"Ma cousine,"* he said. *"Ma cousine americaine."*

The concierge smiled his knowing smile a little bit more knowingly and waved us on. Whatever he thought we were up to was at least permitted in this hotel. I began to giggle. Marty cupped his hand over my mouth as we ascended the first flight of stairs. His room was on the fourth floor. My shoes bit hard into the back of my heels and I removed them for the rest of the climb.

The room was small but I noticed right away the overstuffed armchair in which it would not be impossible to spend the night. The narrow bed was covered with a grotesquely gaudy floral patterned spread of mauves and pinks. Heavy ruffled olive green drapes hung over one window, and a huge armoire loomed menacingly over everything. Marty turned on two lamps, which put out a glow only slightly brighter than one candle. "See you next week," he said, his face taking on the color of the drapes, and he disappeared inside the bathroom.

Dropping my shoes, I sank into the chair and rested my sore and bleeding feet upon a valise. Then I noticed the bidet. I filled it with warm water, pushed the chair beside it, sat down again and immersed my feet. What comfort! The pinches of pain quieted, the blisters soothed. I pushed the drapes aside and looked out the open window onto the dark blue night sky. Across the street were the tightly shuttered windows of apartments, and behind them a large crane rose over the rooftops, poised for action. I saw a corner of the bakery down the block and caught the faintest smell of yeast dough riding on the air that rippled in, warm and velvety, from the night. The sweetest and gentlest of breezes lapped in through the window with little waves of laughter from a café, melodious waves of an opera from a radio somewhere, waves of éclairs and apple tarts, subtle waves of brininess from the Seine: they all rode in on the breeze when I pulled aside the drapes, bathing me in the delicious melancholy of a summer night in Paris. I felt a lump in my throat and, in my eyes, a sting of sentimental tears. For the briefest instant I forgot heartbreak and pain, and this world seemed momentarily to be joined with another, unknown to us, the exquisiteness of which could only be intimated in the breeze of such a night. That was the world where men and women experienced true and everlasting love with one another and children had no dread or need of punishment and there was no such thing as death. A tear rolled down my cheek. I thought I had long ago outgrown the notion of that world and that the longing for it had disappeared with other childish hopes. But a whiff of Paris air on a silky night brought it back for just a second.

I gazed at the rooftops. City of light, city of love. What did we know of love, Marty and I, and where did we ever learn it? I had learned that love was not just knowing whether to make lamb chops or pot roast. But it was also not pinning your hopes on the impossible or being swept off your feet by a dark and handsome charmer, either. No. There had to be something in between.

"Why didn't they ever teach us about what was in between?" I muttered. Or were we destined simply to yearn for it on summer evenings?

"Huh?" Marty called out weakly from the bathroom.

"Nothing," I said. "I'm talking to myself."

"Huh?"

"Forget it!" I hollered.

The water got cold. I rested my shriveled feet on the valise, then leaned my head back, closed my eyes, and let the breeze of perfection waft gently across my face. I must have fallen asleep for a minute or two; the sound of the toilet flushing woke me. I opened my eyes and watched Marty stagger out, his face ghostly. He threw himself onto the bed.

"I had to come all the way to Paris for this?" he croaked.

"You could have gone to Mexico," I replied.

He groaned, sat up, and with great effort removed his shoes and socks, then fell onto his back again. He fumbled behind his head, pulled out a small cushion, and threw it weakly in my direction. "Here, make yourself at home."

I stretched out as best I could in the chair. How sad we were: my cousin the world traveler, prostrate on his bed; me, the cosmopolitan expatriate, exhausted and homeless, trying to sleep in a chair. There we were, fond cousins, drunk, sick, and in pain.

"Oooh," moaned Marty. He turned off the lamps.

"Uh-huh," I said in feeble commiseration. The bulb in the hall stairway went on, sending a narrow shaft of light under the door, then went off. We must have each drifted into a fitful doze for a few minutes. Then I heard him stir. "Marty?" I called out.

"Huh?"

"It'll be all right, won't it?"

"Sure." He paused a minute. "You'll walk again and I'll eat food again."

"No, I don't mean that. I mean everything."

A few chords of music came in through the window, followed by quiet. Then came voices: a man, a woman, a giggle. A low murmur, quiet, and finally a long, sensuous ripple of laughter, a woman's laughter. I felt the lump in my throat again. I sighed. "Marty?"

"Yeah?"

"It can all be happy and new again, can't it?"

"What can?"

I smelled the yeast again. "Like children."

"Like what children?"

The aroma of croissants blew in, fragrant on the nighttime air. I took the yeasty sweet smell of baking deep into my lungs.

"Like nevertheless," I said.

"Nevertheless," he repeated sleepily, then snorted laughter back through his nose. We both chuckled to ourselves.

"Krupwinger galutnik."

"Zip zie," he murmured.

I changed position in the chair, stretched my legs further, and felt a gentle, unexpected peacefulness overtake me. The night was absolutely quiet: no laughter, no music, no sound on the stairway, no traffic, no Metro, not even the klaxon of a distant taxi, but only, now, a series of stuffy snores from Marty, the gruff and rhythmic tune of his repose.

ACKNOWLEDGMENTS

Stories in this book were originally published, in slightly different forms, in *The Georgia Review* ("The Story"), *Indiana Review* ("The Menorah Girl"), *Witness* ("Josephine's Release"), and *Glimmer Train Stories* ("Bobbi and Loretta"). Excerpts from "Open Season" appeared in *Fiction*.

The title story of this collection was originally chosen as "Best Novella" in a literary contest adminstered by the staff of Scala House. The judge of the contest was Jana Harris, University of Washington teacher, and author of several works of fiction and poetry, including *Oh How Can I Keep On Singing?* and the forthcoming *We Never Speak Of It: Idaho-Wyoming Poems 1889* (both from Ontario Review Press). The publisher would like to acknowledge Jana for her dilligence and keen judgment in introducing Lucy Honig's work to us.

ABOUT LUCY HONIG

LUCY HONIG'S WORK HAS APpeared widely in such publications as *DoubleTake, Ploughshares, Georgia Review, Witness,* and *Glimmer Train Stories.* Her stories were selected on two occasions for the O. Henry Awards (1992 and 1996), and once for inclusion in the *Best American Short Stories* (1988). Her first collection of short fiction, *The Truly Needy and Other Stories,* won the 1999 Drue Heinz Literature Prize and was published by University of Pittsburgh Press. She lives in eastern Massachusetts and teaches at Boston University.